RETURN TO CHRISTMAS

A CONTEMPORARY NOVEL

KATHI MACIAS

AWARD-WINNING AUTHOR

OTHER FICTION TITLES BY
KATHI MACIAS

"QUILT" SERIES
The Moses Quilt
The Doctor's Christmas Quilt
The Singing Quilt

"FREEDOM" SERIES
Deliver Me from Evil
Special Delivery
The Deliverer

"EXTREME DEVOTION" SERIES
More Than Conquerors
No Greater Love
Red Ink
The People of the Book

CHRISTMAS BOOKS
A Christmas Gift
A Christmas Journey Home: Miracle in the Manger
Unexpected Christmas Hero

RETURN TO

CHRISTMAS

A CONTEMPORARY NOVEL

KATHI MACIAS

AWARD-WINNING AUTHOR

NEW HOPE®
PUBLISHERS
Gospel-Centered. Missions-Driven.

BIRMINGHAM, ALABAMA

New Hope® Publishers
PO Box 12065
Birmingham, AL 35202-2065
NewHopePublishers.com
New Hope Publishers is a division of WMU®.

New Hope Publishers serves its authors as they express their
views, which may not express the views of the publisher.

Library of Congress Cataloging-in-Publication Data
Macias, Kathi, 1948-
        Return to Christmas : a novel / Kathi Macias.
        pages cm
        ISBN 978-1-59669-442-2 (sc)
1. Christmas stories. 2. Christian fiction. I. Title.
        PS3563.I42319R48 2015
        813'.54--dc23
                        2015021196

ISBN-10: 1-59669-442-4
ISBN-13: 978-1-59669-442-2

N154120 • 1015 • 2.5M1

RETURN TO CHRISTMAS

PROLOGUE

*S*and. Why did there have to be so much sand? At times Chet Mason suspected it was in his food; other times he was certain of it.

He glanced at his friend and fellow Marine, Todd Bishop, who stood less than fifty feet away. Their guard duty would end in less than an hour. Chet knew Todd would make a beeline for some chow; the guy was always hungry. After considering the very real possibility of sand in their food, however, Chet wasn't so sure it was worth it. Besides, the lure of sleep was stronger. He'd been up for nearly thirty-six hours, and all he wanted now was some serious shut-eye.

Todd must have felt Chet's gaze, as he turned his head and offered a smile. "Hey, Sarge," he teased, "don't tell me we've been here so long that I'm starting to look good to you."

Chet chuckled. "Never happen, Bishop. Your ugly mug's the reason they call us Jarheads."

Todd scarcely had time to shake his head and grin before a white-hot explosion rocked their world. The next thing Chet knew, he was facedown in the dirt, wondering if his ears had been blown off. He couldn't hear a thing.

CHAPTER 1

*T*he early fall morning was cool and damp, but Chet didn't mind. Weather had become nearly irrelevant to him over the last few years. Besides, when you lived in Southern California, who could complain about a little fog or rain? Ninety percent of the time the weather allowed for almost any outdoor activity imaginable. The only negative aspect of today's damp forecast for him was that it made it that much easier to slip deeper into the dark mood that seemed to take a bigger bite out of him every day.

Chet almost smiled as he watched his three-year-old plow his toy truck through the sand. Kevin hadn't lived nearly long enough to know that sand wasn't always a welcome playground—and Chet hoped it would stay that way. He wanted more than anything for his own combat experiences to pay the price to help secure a safe and productive future for Kevin, one where the now innocent child wouldn't have to learn how to kill people. Sadly, Chet doubted that would be the case.

"Daddy! Come and play with me."

Chet refocused and realized his son was watching him with wide blue eyes and an expectant smile. A sandbox was the last place Chet wanted to hang out, but there was nothing he wouldn't do to spend bonding time with Kevin. He'd missed out on far too much of his child's first three years of life, and he was going to do everything possible to make it up to him now.

He rose from the hard, cold metal bench and crossed the short distance to the spot where Kevin waited. The little boy's smile expanded, and his eyes danced with anticipation as he watched his father approach.

This, Chet thought, is what it's all about. It's why I survived two deployments to the Middle East. To keep him safe. All of it...to keep him safe.

JENEEN PRAYED she hadn't made a mistake. She'd tried so hard to hold out, to find another way. But the bills were overdue, including the house payment, and there seemed little promise that Chet would land a permanent job anytime soon. They couldn't afford to wait any longer.

"Good morning, Mr. Johnson." She smiled at the customer who'd become familiar in the short two weeks she'd worked at the bank. "What can I help you with today?"

The elderly man with bushy eyebrows slid his transaction from his side of the counter to hers as he began a lengthy explanation of why he needed to withdraw forty dollars. Jeneen knew he'd been in just a few days earlier to make a similar withdrawal; she also knew he could easily make the withdrawal at the ATM outside. But the man was obviously lonely and enjoyed having someone to talk to, even if it was a bank teller he scarcely knew.

As Jeneen took care of the transaction, breaking the cash into fives and ones as he requested, Mr. Johnson droned on about his need to go to the grocery store to pick up fresh fruit. She counted out his withdrawal and asked if there was anything else she could do for him.

The rheumy eyes stared at her for a moment, and he looked as if he were about to ask for something. She waited, but then he shook his head. "No, nothing else," he said, his smile fading as he spoke. "Thank you."

"And thank you, Mr. Johnson. Have a nice day."

He nodded and stepped away from the counter to allow the next customer in line to take his place.

Even as Jeneen prepared to greet the young woman with two toddlers sleeping in a double stroller, she watched the hunched shoulders and shuffling steps of a man she sensed must be lonely beyond imagining.

I was lonely both times Chet was gone for all those long months at a time, but I had hope that he'd return. And at least I had Kevin to keep me company. She sighed, wondering if Mr. Johnson had anyone to help ease the loneliness in his life.

She pulled her attention back to her current customer, who wanted to make a small deposit into her checking account and also to get change for a couple of twenties. By the time Jeneen finished both transactions, the two little ones in the stroller were waking up and beginning to fuss.

"Almost lunchtime for them," the woman said, her face weary and even apologetic as the children's level of fussing grew louder. "Guess I'd better get them home and feed them before they really cut loose and drive everyone crazy."

Jeneen smiled. "Don't worry about it. I have a three-year-old."

"Only one?"

Jeneen nodded, wondering why she suddenly felt the need to apologize for not having more.

"You're smart," the woman said. "Lucky, too. We only wanted one, at least for now, but we got twins." She sighed. "Two of them and not enough of me."

She put her change and deposit slip into her wallet then stuffed the wallet into the diaper bag that hung from the stroller handle. Jeneen wished her a good day, and the young mother steered the stroller toward the front doors.

At least you're with them, Jeneen had wanted to say. *You're not at work while someone else takes care of your child.*

But of course she didn't say that. She felt guilty for even thinking it. But the fact was that Jeneen hated leaving Kevin at daycare, even though he seemed to be adjusting.

At least he's with Chet today, she thought, locking her cash box to take her scheduled break. She placed the "next window" sign on the counter in front of her and wondered if she should call Chet while she had a few spare moments.

She wanted to know everything was all right at home and maybe even have a chance to hear Kevin's voice, but she knew Chet sometimes took offense at her calls during the day.

"Don't you think I can take care of my own son?" he'd challenged the last time she'd called when Kevin was with Chet for the day. "You don't have to micro-manage every minute of my life, you know."

The words had cut to her heart. Why was he so defensive? She'd noticed a little of that the first time he'd come home from deployment, but this time it seemed worse. Was it because he'd opted not to re-enlist? They'd decided together that four years was enough and it was time for him to re-enter civilian life so he could be home with his family. But the re-entry wasn't going as planned.

Jeneen entered the break room and poured herself a cup of stale coffee before taking a seat at one of the three small round tables spaced out around the room. She was pleased to have the break room to herself as she kicked off her shoes and massaged her right foot. *I don't mind working again, but I do mind having to put Kevin in daycare. I wanted so much to stay home with him for a couple more years.*

She sighed and took a sip of coffee. It tasted every bit as awful as she'd expected. No doubt hours old by now.

I wonder what they're doing. Chet said he might take Kevin to the park. I hope he remembered his jacket. I wouldn't want Kevin to get sick.

Fighting tears she pulled her cellphone from her purse and hit the speed dial. Chet might get upset, but she needed to be sure her baby was OK.

CHET'S CELLPHONE rang, and he pulled it from his pocket to confirm it was Jeneen. When he'd checked the screen, he shoved the phone back in his pocket and let the call go to voicemail. He loved his wife and was truly glad to be home with her again, but at least in Afghanistan he had something to do each day. Since he'd left the Marine Corps a few months earlier, the only work he'd found was with a construction company who called him now and then when they needed an extra hand. The money was good when he worked, but it was never steady and had no benefits.

How many applications do I have to fill out? And how many humiliating interviews do I have to endure before I find a real job? He shook his head. He'd been to the VA and availed himself of a counselor who was supposed to help him find employment, but so far that was another dead end. When Jeneen told him she was going back to work, it had been the last straw. He knew his wife wanted to stay home and take care of Kevin, and it's what he wanted for her too. But apparently she was much better at finding a job than he was because within a few days of filling out her first applications, she'd been hired.

He looked at his son, whose head was bent down as he filled the back of his truck with sand. His blond curls lay in unruly ringlets as he concentrated on his task. In all honesty he couldn't fault Jeneen for taking the job. She and Kevin needed health care, and his military benefits covered only himself. But once she'd landed a job, they'd had no choice but to enroll Kevin in daycare since they never knew when the construction company would call Chet to a job for a few days. At least he was able to take care of Kevin on the days he wasn't working, though he suspected his wife was more comfortable with their son being cared for by professionals than by his own father.

"Daddy?"

Chet pulled his attention back to his child and forced a smile. "What is it, buddy?"

The boy looked very serious. "Are you sad, Daddy?"

Chet caught his breath. That's all he needed—to have his son feeling sorry for him. He shook his head and widened his smile. "No, son. Daddy's not sad. Just a little tired, that's all."

The child's face brightened. "We could go home and take a nap."

Chet's heart melted. How could he possibly resent anything that allowed him to spend time with his son? All those long months away when he'd wondered how Kevin was doing and wished they could be together...

"Tell you what," he said. "Let's go home and make some sandwiches first, and then after lunch we'll take a nap together."

"Peanut butter?"

Chet laughed. "Yeah, sure. Peanut butter."

Kevin clapped his chubby hands, and Chet lifted the boy from the sand and carried him to the bench to brush off his pants and empty his shoes. It wouldn't do for Jeneen to come home after working all day and find sand everywhere.

CHAPTER 2

*A*s Chet headed for work, he noted that the weather had once again changed quickly and drastically, as it often did in their little SoCal corner of the world. The early-morning fog that had hung around the past few days had been blown back to sea by the prevailing Santa Anas, or East Winds, as the longtime residents called them. Hot and dry, they roared into the area several times a year, primarily in the fall as they had done this time. In this drought-stricken area of the world, they were not a welcome arrival.

Chet was bothered by the Santa Anas for many reasons, not the least of which was their reminder of his time in Afghanistan, something he'd like to block out completely but didn't seem able to do. But he had no problem understanding why some people called them "devil winds." Not just people but even animals seemed more restless than usual when the dry winds blew. But at least they were temporary, he reminded himself, never lasting more than a few days at a time. Today he would do his best to ignore them and concentrate instead on being grateful he'd been called out on a job that might last several days.

He pulled into the dirt parking lot next to the jobsite and eased his five-year-old Dodge pickup into the only remaining parking space. He recognized a couple of the vehicles already there and knew he'd be working with a few familiar faces. More than once the guys had tried to strike up a conversation with him, but he'd closed them off, not yet ready to risk new relationships, however inconsequential they might be.

Chet turned off the engine and started to reach across the seat to grab his lunch sack but stopped, suddenly feeling a bit lightheaded and short of breath. He put both hands on the top of the steering wheel and lowered his head to rest on top of them, all the while taking deep breaths and trying to focus on a peaceful garden setting as he'd done so many times in Afghanistan. What he couldn't figure out was why he continued to need to do such a thing now that he was no longer living in a dangerous place.

A rap on the driver's-side window jerked him back to attention, and he felt his heart race and his eyes go wide as he turned his head toward the sound. One of the guys he'd worked with a couple times since being home grinned at him. "Hey, Mason," he called out. "You gonna stay in there all day or come out here and go to work with the rest of us?"

Chet swallowed, taking one last deep breath to try to calm his heart, and did his best to return a smile. "Yeah, sure. On my way," he mumbled, trying to remember the guy's name. He grabbed his lunch and climbed out of the truck, hit the lock button, and pocketed the keys as he fell into step with the guy whose name he couldn't remember .

"LOOKS LIKE the new boy, Kevin, is making friends."

Breanna Pritchard lifted her gaze from her own three-year-old who sat in his usual corner of the yard, stacking blocks by himself, to focus on the trio of boys playing on the slide. For the most part they took turns climbing up and then zipping down, with hair flying and squeals of joy adding to the rest of the noise on the busy playground. Breanna smiled and nodded.

"He sure does," she agreed, her smile wistful. If only her own son, Ryan, could bond as easily as the other children his age. But then, she reminded herself, Ryan wasn't like the other children, and both she and Steve had understood and accepted that possibility from the beginning.

She refused to let her thoughts go there—again—and turned to her young assistant, Dani Martin, who stood beside her. Together they kept an eye on the various activities and watched for any potential problems. Breanna had been through several teacher's aides in the five years since she'd opened Sun Valley Preschool and Daycare, and Dani was definitely one of her favorites.

"So how's everything going with you?" she asked, genuinely interested. "School? Friends?" She paused and grinned. "Romance?"

Dani turned her eyes from the children to Breanna only long enough to flash a smile and shake her head before looking back toward the playground. "I was wondering how long it would take you to ask about all that this week. It's Wednesday already, and this is your first mention of it. You're slipping."

Breanna laughed. She'd expected such a response but knew she could get away with it. Dani was very open about nearly every aspect of her life, including and especially her Christian faith, which had been the glue that quickly cemented Breanna and Dani's growing friendship. And because both Breanna and Dani still attended the same church where they'd first met, their relationship had continued to deepen, particularly as Breanna observed Dani's active involvement in both the children's and singles' ministries. Though Dani was nearly ten years younger than Breanna, and single, neither those facts nor their employer-employee relationship had caused any distance between them.

"Well?" Breanna prodded. "Are you going to tell me or not?"

Dani chuckled, her long blonde hair pulled back in a ponytail and held in place by a multi-colored Scrunchie. The girl wore only a smidgen of lipstick and dressed modestly but practically, though that had done little to discourage the attention she regularly received from male admirers.

"School's fine," she said, her eyes still scanning the playground. "I've got a long way to go yet, but I'm going to get my degree one of these days. It makes for a crazy schedule, working here all day and then going to classes four nights a week plus doing a ton of homework on top of it, but I wouldn't trade it for anything. Meanwhile, I love my job and all the experience I'm getting right here."

Breanna nodded. "On-the-job training. You're going to make a fantastic teacher one of these days."

"I hope so." Dani shot another quick glance at Breanna, her warm brown eyes smiling for just an instant before turning back to the children. "And as for friends, that's all good. As you know, I mostly hang out with my two long-time friends from church." She shrugged. "We manage to get together at least once a week in spite of our busy schedules. We go to a movie or out for pizza...or just sit and talk and listen to music." She shrugged. "It's enough."

"As far as your girlfriends go, sure. But you didn't give me an update on the romance part of your life. Last time I dragged it out of you, there was someone special you'd just met and thought it had possibilities of growing into...something." She raised her eyebrows. "So? Is it?"

Dani once again directed her gaze to the playground. "Is it what?"

Dani's question was nothing more than a dodge, Breanna knew, but she played along. "Is it turning into 'something'?" She leaned closer and said, "Inquiring minds want to know."

That evoked an outright laugh from Dani. "You're impossible, you know that?"

"Maybe," Breanna said. "But that's beside the point. What's up with this new relationship?"

Dani sighed and turned toward Breanna, this time holding her gaze. "His name is Mike. I met him at an inter-church concert, which I think I already mentioned . . ."

Breanna nodded, and Dani continued.

"He's a strong believer. He works at the hardware store around the corner from the church, and he's taking classes at the Bible college sponsored by our church because he wants to become a youth minister. And yes, he's absolutely, positively gorgeous."

Breanna was in full-attention mode now. "And the relationship is developing as you thought it would...?"

Dani smiled and nodded. "Yeah, it is. Neither of us is at a place in our lives when we can think about anything serious or long-term, but we're spending time together and seeing each other when we can." She shrugged. "That's it . . . in a nutshell. My entire life. Fascinating enough to make a movie about it, don't you think?"

Breanna laughed. "Sounds good to me. For someone barely twenty years old, I think you're right on target. In fact, I—"

A scream pierced the air, interrupting their discussion. Both women turned to see two four-year-old girls who seemed to want to play together all the time but never made it through an hour without at least one very loud dispute. The girls were now pulling on the same jump-rope. Their argument grew louder as Breanna and Dani headed in their direction.

"I had it first," one declared, pulling on one end of the rope.

The other girl shook her head, pulling just as hard on the other end. "But it's my turn. I never get a turn!"

"Back to reality," Dani declared, squatting down to talk to one of the girls.

"Amen," Breanna agreed, leaning over.

JENEEN WAS always relieved to finally get off work and head to the preschool-daycare to pick up Kevin. She reminded herself regularly that he was in good hands and was having an opportunity to socialize and make friends., He was verbal for a three-year-old, and he adapted to new people and settings fairly easily, but her heart still broke every time she left him in the mornings.

She walked in the main entrance and smiled at the bright, colorful motif of children's artwork that covered the windows and walls. A group of little ones sat on tiny plastic chairs at a long table, playing with clay as a woman with a long blonde ponytail somehow managed to sit in one of the impossibly small chairs with them, complimenting and encouraging them while they worked.

Another group of children danced and sang in a corner of the large room, following instructions from another teacher's aide as she showed them how to pose in a certain way, to jump up and down, and to wave their hands high in the air, all in time to the music.

Kevin wasn't in either group, so she headed for the playground, knowing some of the children would be outside running off some late-afternoon energy. Sure enough, she spotted him playing on the slide.

Apparently Kevin spotted her as well, for he quickly climbed to the top and cried, "Mom, watch me!" Then he slid down to the bottom, landing in the soft sand that surrounded the slide.

She waved at him as she approached. "That was wonderful, Kevin. Really good!"

He beamed, his blond curls damp with sweat—and no doubt full of sand. Ah well, that's what baths were for.

"I can go faster," Kevin declared, obviously excited to have an audience. "Watch me again!"

She watched him twice more before she decided it was time to sign him out so they could go home.

"Mrs. Mason?"

A familiar voice caught her just before she called out to Kevin to tell him it was time to leave. Jeneen turned to the smiling face of Breanna Pritchard, the school's director.

"Hello, Mrs. Pritchard," Jeneen said, returning her smile. The woman's green eyes and light skin went perfectly with her short red curls. Jeneen imagined they were close to the same age. She thought the woman was striking, warm, friendly, as well as patient and calm—the perfect combination for such a job.

"Please, call me Breanna, will you? May I call you Jeneen?"

Jeneen smiled. "Absolutely. I'd like that." She cast a quick glance toward the slide, just long enough to confirm that Kevin still played there, along with a handful of other children. "So how's Kevin doing? He seems to like it here."

Breanna nodded. "He sure does. And he's making friends quickly. Seems to get along well with just about all the children. And, as you can see, he absolutely loves the slide."

Jeneen smiled. "He's always had that easy-going personality, a lot like his father used to. . . ." Her voice trailed off, and she felt her face grow warm. "Anyway, thank you for the encouraging words. It's good to know he's doing well."

"And I have no doubt he'll continue to do well," Breanna agreed. "Some children adapt easier than others, and he seems to be one of them."

A frown creased Breanna's brow then, as a sense of what appeared to Jeneen to be concern flashed in her eyes. "Is...everything all right?" Jeneen asked. "Is there a problem with Kevin?"

Breanna's frown quickly smoothed out, and her eyes opened wide. "Oh no," she said quickly, shaking her head. "Absolutely not. Kevin is an absolute delight—no problems whatsoever. I was just..." Her voice trailed off for a moment as her gaze traveled across the playground toward a boy playing by himself in a corner. "I was actually thinking about Ryan, my . . . my son." She smiled, though it appeared somewhat forced. "He's three years old too."

"How nice! Do you have other children?"

Breanna's smile faded, and she shook her head. "No. Just Ryan."

"And is he here? I'd love to meet him. No doubt he and Kevin have already gotten acquainted."

Breanna shook her head again. "I doubt it. Ryan isn't very . . . sociable." She indicated the lone figure playing in the corner. "That's him over there."

Jeneen started to ask if she could meet him, but she sensed it was best to let it go. She nodded. "I know how three-year-olds can be. One minute they love something or someone, and the next minute they lose interest and move on to something else." She shrugged. "I think it's just the age, don't you?"

Breanna hesitated. "Could be," she said then glanced at the slide. "Looks like Kevin is in his favorite place with his two favorite friends. Those three boys are becoming insepa-rable and want to play on the slide every chance they get." She smiled. "You'll have to excuse me, Jeneen. I need to go relieve one of the aides."

"Of course." Jeneen watched her walk away. Then she turned back to Kevin and called him to her side. "Now," she said as he opened his mouth to protest. "We have to go home and see Daddy."

The child's face lit up, and he raced toward her from the slide. It was time to go home, and that was something the child was always ready to do if he knew his daddy would be there waiting for him.

CHAPTER 3

As much as she hated to do it, Jeneen stopped at a fast-food place on the way home. She hated stretching their budget any tighter than it already was, but she was too tired to cook, and Chet probably was too. She rolled down her window to place her order, determined to limit it to broiled chicken and salad.

"I want fries and ketchup," Kevin announced from his car seat in the back. "That's my favorite."

Jeneen ignored him and placed her order.

"You forgot the fries and ketchup," Kevin said, his voice a notch louder this time. "And soda. I want soda."

Jeneen pressed the window button and waited until the window shut all the way before turning back to her son. "I'm sorry, sweetheart," she said, "but no fries or sodas tonight. We need to eat something healthy so you can grow up to be big and strong." She smiled and waited for a response.

Kevin's blue eyes began to shine. "Like Daddy?"

Jeneen nodded. "Yes, like Daddy. You'd like that, wouldn't you?"

Kevin nodded and grinned.

"That's why we have to eat healthy. Fries and sodas aren't healthy."

Kevin's grin faded, and his eyes grew serious. "Daddy eats fries. When he takes me for lunch, we always have fries. And sodas too."

If she didn't know better, she'd think her son wore a "gotcha" look. But he was too young for that . . . wasn't he?

She shook her head. "Maybe Daddy ordered fries and sodas because he forgot about the healthy part. I'll talk to him about it later."

The child's mouth turned down at the sides. "No more fries and sodas with Daddy?"

She sighed. "No more fries and sodas with Mommy or Daddy—unless it's a very special occasion."

Kevin's smile was back, and his eyes were dancing again. "Today's a special 'casion, so we can have fries and soda."

She kept her voice calm as she pulled up even with the pick-up window. "Today is not a special occasion, Kevin. Special occasions don't happen very often. Now let's talk about something else." She hit the button to lower the window and reached out to exchange her money for the food. By the time she'd completed the transaction and placed the bag of food on the floor of the passenger side, she could see Kevin's pout in the rearview mirror.

This was out of character for him, though she knew children went through stages. But Kevin had never argued or pouted when he didn't get his way—not until Chet came home. She had to admit, she'd seen flashes of a bad attitude developing in Kevin since then. Was it possible her husband's moodiness was beginning to rub off on their son?

"So, Kevin," she said, smiling at him in the mirror, "it looks like you've made some new friends at school."

The child perked up immediately, and he nodded, his short blond curls bouncing and his blue eyes coming back to life. "I have two best friends. James and Mark play on the slide with me all the time."

Jeneen breathed a sigh of relief. This was the Kevin she was used to—easygoing, friendly, never nursing a grudge, and seldom demanding his own way. "That's wonderful," she said, matching her level of enthusiasm to his. "Tell me about James and Mark and all the fun things you do together."

As Kevin chattered away, Jeneen covered the remaining few blocks home. When she hit the garage door opener on her sun visor and pulled into the garage, she saw that Chet's truck wasn't there yet. *Must be working overtime. That's great! We can use the extra money.*

She helped Kevin out of the car and unlocked the door that would let them into the kitchen. Then she went back and opened the front passenger door to grab the food. That grilled chicken smelled wonderful, and it had been far too long since lunch. And as much as she knew they needed the extra money, she hoped Chet wouldn't be much longer. She liked it when they could all eat together, but for now she'd just set his food aside and reheat it in the microwave when she heard his truck pull in.

FROM HIS vantage point on a side street where he'd stopped at a stop sign, Chet had seen Jeneen's car go by. No doubt she and Kevin were already in the house by now. He wondered what she was fixing for dinner. Had Kevin asked for him yet? In so many ways, he knew his wife and child had welcomed him home and readjusted their lives to fit him in. But he couldn't miss the occasional resentment that flared up when it seemed he overstepped his bounds. Was he just imagining it, or were there times when one or both of them resented his return and missed the life they'd had when he was gone?

He shook his head. What was wrong with him? When it was cool and cloudy, he blamed his depression on the weather. When these devil winds blew hot and dry, he blamed them for the unnamed agitation that gnawed at his soul. Why didn't he just snap out of it and get on with his life? He was finally home where he'd longed to be every day and night of his deployments. So why didn't he feel like he was home? Why couldn't things go back to the way they were . . . before?

Before what? he asked himself. *Before my deployments? Before I saw so much death and destruction? Before I hardened my heart to try to get through it?*

A flash of white blasted his brain, and he shut his eyes. He wasn't about to let himself start thinking about Todd. No way was he wasn't going there.

He took a deep breath and took his foot off the brake. Obviously he couldn't sit here all night. He may as well go home and see his family.

JENEEN HAD just sat down at the kitchen table with Kevin when she heard the garage door opening.

"Daddy's home!" Kevin's grin warmed her heart. It sure hadn't taken him long to reattach to his father. She returned her son's smile. After all, wasn't having Chet back home what she'd hoped and prayed for all those months? She'd even kept his memory alive in Kevin's heart by showing him their handsome Marine's picture every day and telling the child how much his daddy loved him.

She stood and went to open the kitchen door to greet her husband. He was just climbing out of his truck when their eyes connected.

He smiled, though she sensed it was forced. Was he tired? Did he feel all right? Why did she always feel as if she had to walk on eggshells with him?

He embraced her briefly and bent to plant a kiss on her forehead before he stepped inside. She noticed his smile broadened when he saw Kevin.

"Daddy!" Kevin's grin was ear-to-ear. "We have chicken!"

Chet actually chuckled. "So I see." He nodded. "It looks good."

"It is," Kevin agreed, but his grin faded before he spoke again. "But we got salad. Mom said no fries or sodas 'cause they're not good for us."

Chet went to the sink and washed his hands, speaking to them with his back turned. "Your mom's right. Fries and sodas aren't good for us."

"But you like 'em, Daddy. And you always get 'em for us."

Chet shut off the water and turned around to face them as he dried his hands on a dishtowel. His smile was gone, and his face looked flushed. "I was wrong to do that," he mumbled. "Next time I'll get us salad instead. Now let's eat. I'm hungry." He tossed the dishtowel on the counter and joined his family at the table.

CHAPTER 4

*I*t's ridiculous," Jeneen lamented as she talked on the phone with her mother-in-law. "It's not even Halloween yet, and already I'm seeing signs for Christmas layaway specials."

Celia Mason sighed, loud enough that Jeneen couldn't miss it. "I know what you mean," Celia said. "When Chet was little, stores didn't put up Halloween decorations until at least the end of September or even the first of October. And in between Halloween and Christmas, Thanksgiving was the big push. Now it seems they go straight from back-to-school specials to Christmas. I'm always sad to see how commercialized Christmas has become."

Jeneen agreed with her mother-in-law, as she did on nearly everything. The woman was the absolute mold-breaker when it came to countering the interfering or annoying in-law stereotype. Celia had been widowed after two short years of marriage, so Chet had no real memories of his father. But Jeneen knew Celia had raised her only child in a loving and secure home. It had also been a Christian home, though Chet seemed to have rejected that part of his upbringing once he became an adult. Jeneen and Celia had prayed together at least once a week since Jeneen had become a believer during Chet's first deployment. Their shared faith had cemented an already close relationship, and Jeneen often felt she was closer to Celia than to her own mother.

"It'll be nice having Chet home for Christmas this year, won't it?" Celia said.

Jeneen smiled and nodded, though she knew her mother-in-law couldn't see her. "It sure will. And you'll be joining us again, right?"

"I wouldn't miss it," Celia said. "And I appreciate more than you know that you've always included me in your holiday celebrations, even when Chet was gone." She sighed again. "Seems the holidays are the toughest times when you're alone."

Alone. Jeneen hadn't been alone at the holidays when Chet was gone—she'd had Kevin, after all, and Celia too. Not to mention her own family, though she didn't have many warm holiday memories of her growing-up years and therefore didn't feel drawn to visit her family on special occasions.

As if she could read Jeneen's mind, Celia said, "And speaking of being alone for the holidays, are you going to invite your parents for Christmas this year?"

Jeneen squirmed. She knew she'd been skating on thin ice when she allowed the conversation to touch on the upcoming holidays. Her mother-in-law felt strongly that all holidays, particularly Christmas, should be centered around family, and no one should be left out. As a matter of fact, the two of them had talked about this very thing just last year—and the year before. And always Jeneen gave Celia the same answer.

"I . . . haven't really worked out the details yet, Mom, so I haven't mentioned it to them. I . . . suppose I should invite them."

"Of course you should." Her voice softened. "I know you and your parents have had your differences, sweetheart, but—"

"They're not really my parents," Jeneen said, interrupting Celia mid-sentence. "I mean, my mother is, of course, but Pete's only my stepdad, and you know we're not close."

"I do know that, yes. But it doesn't have to be that way—especially now."

Zing. As kind and gentle as her mother-in-law could be, she knew just how to deliver an arrow to the heart. The fact that Celia was right didn't make Jeneen feel any better.

Jeneen knew without asking that Celia was referring to the fact that Jeneen was a Christian now and had no business carrying hurts or slights from the past. True, neither her mother nor Pete had ever physically abused her, but Jeneen and her sister, Marilyn, had always known they weren't priorities in their family. And now even Marilyn was gone. . . .

"Jeneen? Are you there?"

She shook her head. She had to stop drifting off that way. "Yes, I'm . . . I'm here. Sorry." She cleared her throat. "You know, Mom, I really have to go. It's Saturday, and I have so much to do around here to make up for being away all week."

"I hope you're having Chet help you. You can't work full-time and take care of everything else too, you know."

"I know, Mom. And he does help . . . when he can. But he's working today, so I don't want to dump too much on him when he gets home. It's been a full week of work, and we're grateful for the money."

"Of course you are. But I just don't want you taking on more than—"

Jeneen jumped in before this conversation took on a life of its own. "Sorry, Mom. I have to go. I hear Kevin calling me. I guess naptime's over for today. I'll talk to you later."

She hung up with a sigh and headed for her son's room, grateful for the little boy's perfect timing.

KEVIN WAS sitting up in bed when Jeneen walked in. His face was flushed and puffy from sleep, and he clutched his favorite blanket, holding the tattered satiny binding against his cheek as he'd done nearly all his short life. His blond curls were damp with perspiration, and his lashes seemed wet. Had he been crying?

"Is everything OK, baby?" she asked, sitting down next to him on the bed. "Did you have a bad dream?"

The little boy nodded and snuggled up against her as she wrapped her arms around him. How was it possible that her precious son could seem so grown up one minute and then revert to his baby habits the next?

She smiled and pressed him closer, his little-boy sleepiness nearly bringing tears to her eyes. Chet had said more than once since he'd been home from his last deployment that Kevin was too old for a "blankie," as the boy called it. He also accused Jeneen of purposely babying him and not letting him grow up. But she didn't agree. After all, she'd been around Kevin a lot more than Chet had, so it was obvious she knew him better. And besides, she loved these special times with her son. Despite Chet's concerns, the growing boy in Kevin would surpass and supplant the baby side of him soon enough. She wasn't ready to give all that up quite yet.

"Tell me about your dream, sweetheart," she whispered into his hair. "Remember, when you have a bad dream, Jesus will help you not be scared anymore. So tell me about it, and then we can pray."

The little boy hiccupped, confirming Jeneen's suspicion that he'd been crying. "I saw a monster," he said, his head nearly buried in her chest. "I think he was going to eat me."

"Poor baby." Jeneen kissed the top of his head. "I know that must have been scary for you, but Jesus isn't going to let any monster eat you."

She smiled and pulled back slightly, then lifted his chin with her finger. "Did you know we all see monsters in our dreams sometimes, even grown-ups?"

His blue eyes widened. "Even you and Daddy?"

"Absolutely. Even me and Daddy. But when I see a monster or feel afraid of anything, I pray, and Jesus makes me feel safe again."

The little boy's forehead drew together in a frown. "But what does Daddy do when he sees a monster? He doesn't talk to Jesus like we do."

Another zing to her heart. First her mother-in-law and now her son. If she wasn't careful to follow her own advice and take her problems to God in prayer, her heart could end up shredded for sure.

"That's true, honey," she said, gently pushing his damp curls back from his face. "But when Daddy was a little boy, your Grandma Mason taught him about Jesus. And one of these days, your daddy is going to start praying again." She smiled. "Until then, you and I can pray for Daddy and ask Jesus to help him. What do you think?"

She could almost see the thoughts swirling around in her child's head. Finally the frown smoothed out, and he smiled. "I think it's a good idea, Mommy." He scrunched his eyes tight, folded his hands together, and waited.

Jeneen's heart warmed at her son's innocence and simple faith. She closed her eyes too.

"Dear Jesus," she began, "thank You for loving us and taking care of us. Thank You that we don't have to be scared of monsters or anything else because You promised to always be with us. So we're asking you now to make the memory of the monster Kevin saw in his dream go away. Heal his heart, Lord, and let him feel the safety of Your presence. And also, Lord, we pray for Kevin's daddy, my husband. We love him very much, Father, and we're so grateful that You brought him back to us safe and sound. But Kevin and I are praying for him now, since he doesn't talk to You himself. We know he probably sees monsters sometimes, just like we do. He gets scared, but he doesn't come and ask for Your help, so we're asking for him. Please, dear God, take away any monsters that might try to scare him and keep him from being happy. Most of all, take away anything that keeps him from seeing how much You love him. We want him to love You like we do. Thank You, Lord."

Before she could continue, Kevin said, "Please don't let any monsters scare Daddy anymore, Jesus. Amen."

"Amen," Jeneen repeated then pulled her son back into an embrace before he could see the tears that had pooled in her own eyes.

SUNDAY MORNING. When Chet and Jeneen first married, Sunday was his favorite day of the week. They'd start it off by sleeping in, and then whoever finally woke up first would get up and make the coffee. If it was football season and the weather was bad, they'd watch the games in bed together. During the rest of the year's bad-weather days, they watched movies. But when the weather was nice—which was often in Southern California—they'd head for the beach and spend a lazy day in the sun and surf.

It wasn't like that anymore, though. Much like it had been when Chet was growing up, Sunday mornings now revolved around getting ready for church. He hadn't minded it so much when he was little and still bought into all that Jesus stuff. But then he hit his teens and knew better. Still, his mom dragged him there despite his protests. One of the best parts of becoming an adult and moving out on his own was that he no longer had to go to church. Marrying someone who didn't care about religion any more than he did was a bonus. But now all that had changed.

He listened to the shower, knowing his wife was getting ready first and would then get Kevin up and ready to go. Thankfully, she had respected his request to stop inviting him, though he could see the longing in her face for him to join them.

Never going to happen, he told himself for the hundredth time.

It was bad enough knowing his wife and mother had teamed up against him. He'd overheard more than one phone conversation between them that ended up being prayer for and about him. He supposed he couldn't stop them from doing that, but he didn't like that they dragged Kevin into it. After all, he was just a kid. And Chet knew all too well what it was like to be a kid forced to attend church every Sunday.

The shower noise stopped. Soon Jeneen would come out of the bathroom and go to the closet to pick out something to wear. He rolled over onto his side with his back to the bathroom door. It was easier to play possum than to deal with her silent invitation for him to join her.

CHAPTER 5

He hadn't meant to go back to sleep, and he would have climbed out of bed and maybe even gone to church with Jeneen if he'd known drifting back off that morning would mean another nightmare. One minute he'd been pretending to be asleep so Jeneen wouldn't ask him to come with her; the next minute he really was asleep, caught in a dream that came all too often these days.

Flashes of light, the sounds and smells of rapid-fire gunfire, the screams of wounded and dying—all flitted through his mind, tugging at his heart and pulling him from a tentative place of safety that he couldn't quite identify. By the time he shot up to a sitting position in bed, blinking at the familiar setting of the bedroom he shared with his wife, he was tangled in the sheets and soaked in sweat.

He buried his head in his hands, taking slow, deep breaths to help calm his heart. How long were these dreams going to continue? He'd hoped they'd fade away after he'd been home for a while, but already Jeneen had been startled awake several times by his thrashing and moaning. And that was the worst part—not being able to hide his nightmares from his wife. What must she think of him? He shook his head. The shell of a man who came home from Afghanistan sure wasn't the same one she sent off months earlier.

He pulled himself from bed and headed for the shower. The least he could do was be up and showered by the time she and Kevin came home. Maybe he'd even have a nice brunch ready for them. His wife loved his scrambled eggs, and Kevin could pack away almost as much bacon as Chet.

Once in the shower, he let the prickly needles of hot water wash away the tension in his neck and shoulders. He knew he should be grateful for getting through two deployments in a war zone with nothing more than a few nightmares and some bad memories, especially when he thought about the price paid by so many of his buddies. But he never imagined it would take so long to get back to normal—whatever that might be. Or was this the new normal of his life—unnamed darkness and memories that haunted his every step?

Right now it took all the concentration he could muster to stay focused on finding a permanent job so he could support his family the way any decent man would want to do. He was just going to have to try harder to push away the memories before they overran him and stole any chance he might have for a productive and positive future.

Jeneen pulled the car into the garage and helped Kevin from the back seat. Still wearing his paper crown from the fast-food restaurant where they'd stopped for lunch on the way home, the little boy appeared to be winding down. *Just might be able to get him down for a nap,* she thought as she opened the door leading into the kitchen.

The smell of bacon greeted her even before they stepped inside. Her heart sank as she took in the breakfast nook, complete with three place-settings, plus covered plates and bowls in the middle of the table, no doubt containing eggs and bacon and who knew what else.

Tears pricked her eyes as she realized her husband had tried to do something nice for them but had no doubt given up by now, since she was nearly an hour late getting home from church.

"I smell bacon!" Kevin ran for the table and lifted the lids off the bowls until he found the bacon. The boy didn't have to be hungry to enjoy his favorite breakfast meat.

He snagged a piece before she could stop him. With dancing eyes, he popped the bacon strip into his mouth, but his face quickly lost its glow. "It's cold," he said, laying the uneaten portion of the strip on the table.

"I know, baby," she said. "Listen, Kev, why don't you go play in your room for a few minutes so Mommy and Daddy can talk, all right?"

Kevin nodded and headed for the hallway while Jeneen breathed a silent prayer that God would help her smooth things over.

HE HEARD them come in, but he refused to leave the bedroom to go greet them. He would stay right where he was, lying on the bed and watching football. They could come to him.

He heard her footsteps, and he tried to refocus on how much he missed his family when he was gone and how happy he should be that he was with them now, but all he could think of was how they'd spoiled his surprise.

Well, technically not "they," since Kevin didn't have much say over what time they got home from church. But Jeneen did, and he didn't see why she couldn't have made a simple phone call to find out what he had planned for the rest of the day. He was relatively sure they'd stopped somewhere to eat while the food he'd prepared for them got cold.

The door opened then, but he kept his eyes glued to the game and its dismal score. Seemed his wife wasn't any more reliable than his favorite team.

"Chet?"

When he didn't respond, she came and sat on the edge of the bed, laying her hand on his arm. He refused to flinch. He'd learned as a Marine how important it was to remain perfectly still, scarcely breathing, in order to avoid the enemy. Was Jeneen his enemy? The question rolled through his mind, but he didn't seem able to come up with an answer.

"Chet, please look at me. I know you can hear me."

A slight catch in her voice told him she was holding back tears.

Stone-faced, he turned his head slightly, allowing their eyes to meet for a split second, just long enough to confirm the hint of tears in her blue eyes. "You're home," he said, diverting his attention back to the TV.

Her pressure on his arm increased slightly. "I'm so sorry. When we left, you were asleep. I had no idea you planned to get up and cook for us." She hesitated before continuing. "It looks delicious. You did a wonderful job."

He refused to let his jaws twitch. Better to let her think her words had no effect.

"Sweetheart," she said, scooting closer on the bed, "why don't we all go in and eat together? It wouldn't take long to warm it up in the microwave, and—"

"Forget it," he growled, continuing to watch his team go down in flames. "I know you've already eaten. I don't need you and Kevin making yourselves sick by eating again. I'll clean it up when this game's over—which shouldn't be long the way things are going."

"Chet, please, listen to me. You're right. We already ate. But I'll put the food in the refrigerator and save it for later. And I'll do the cleanup. It's the least I—"

A quiet knock, followed by the bedroom door opening, interrupted her.

"Hi, Daddy," a cheerful voice called out. "Look what I got!"

Chet's heart twisted. He might be able to ignore his wife, but no way could he hurt the little boy who looked up to him. Besides, none of this was his fault.

He turned and smiled at the towheaded three-year-old. The paper crown on his head identified the stop he and his mother had made on their way home from church.

"Hey, pretty cool hat you got there, buddy."

Kevin scampered over to the bed and hopped up beside his dad. "It's not a hat, Daddy. It's a crown." He took it off and held it up in front of Chet's face. "See? This is where we ate. It's my favorite. And we saw Miss Breanna and Ryan there. His daddy was there too." His grin faded slightly. "I wish you were with us. Maybe we could have had fries and a soda. Mom wouldn't let me."

Chet swallowed a chuckle and shook his head instead. "No, no fries or sodas, remember?" He cut a quick, meaningful glance toward Jeneen. "Mom's orders. And she's the boss, right?"

Kevin ignored the question and put the paper crown back on his head, then settled down next to his father to watch the game. Jeneen sighed and walked out of the room, leaving Chet to curse his bad attitude and wishing things could go back to the way they were before his last deployment.

CHAPTER 6

*B*reanna slipped a cover over Ryan's still form. He always looked so peaceful when he was asleep. And in all fairness, she couldn't say he was rowdy or loud or even curious and playful when he was awake.

She sighed. She had hoped he would come around now that he was in preschool. *He just needs to meet other children,* she'd told herself in the beginning. *It might take him a little longer than normal, but sooner or later he's bound to start bonding with one or two others.*

That was more than a year earlier, not long after Ryan had come home to live with them, and still the small-for-his-age three-year-old kept to himself, preferring to stack blocks in the corner of the playground or hunch over on his mat when playing inside. True, he'd come around to the point that he now allowed Breanna and Steve to hold and even kiss him, but he seldom returned the affection.

She watched him now, curled up on his side, his thumb stuck in his mouth. Steve suggested they should try to break him of the habit, but the social worker had advised against it, assuring them the child would stop on his own when he was ready.

When he feels secure, Breanna thought. *That's what she really meant.* They'd had Ryan for over a year now, and obviously he wasn't yet feeling secure enough to stop sucking his thumb or come to them for love and comfort. Breanna and Steve had to initiate every physical interaction with their son, and though he no longer resisted, neither did he show signs of welcoming it.

Attachment Disorder. The social worker had warned them it could prove to be a lot bigger problem than they might imagine. But she and Steve had been so sure they could love Ryan enough to bring him around.

And we've prayed for him, she reminded herself. *Over and over again. I know You're faithful, God. Please do something to help our son.*

She thought of their chance encounter earlier today when they stopped for lunch after church. They'd no sooner gotten inside than the new boy from her preschool, Kevin Mason, had spotted them.

"Mommy, look," Kevin had cried, a smile spreading across his face. "It's Miss Breanna from my school."

Kevin and his mother had ended up sitting with them as they ate lunch together. Breanna had so hoped that by seating Kevin and Ryan beside one another they would somehow connect. Kevin had even tried more than once to engage Ryan in conversation or play on the small, enclosed playground, but Ryan had acted as if Kevin were invisible. Kevin, of course, had eventually stopped trying and gone on to play without him.

Breanna smiled. She'd discovered that Kevin's mother, Jeneen, was a Christian. They didn't attend the same church, but the more they chatted, the more the two women bonded over their mutual faith and their three-year-olds.

She didn't say much about her husband, Breanna realized then. *I know she has one because he's listed on Kevin's enrollment papers, plus I've heard Kevin talking about him. I wonder how Jeneen would respond if I suggested the six of us get together one day soon.*

The thought warmed her heart, and she got up to leave Ryan to his nap. She knew her husband would be in his recliner, watching football and dozing a bit. Maybe she'd catch him at halftime and see what he thought about the idea of getting to know the Masons. Perhaps that would be the way to finally get Ryan to open up. . . .

CHET HAD stayed in the bedroom for the remainder of Sunday, watching TV and refusing to come out, even to eat supper. Though he seemed to welcome Kevin each time he popped in to visit, Chet limited himself to one-syllable answers with Jeneen.

By bedtime she'd given up trying. She cleaned up the kitchen—including placing the food Chet had made in the refrigerator in case he wanted it at some point—and then put Kevin to bed before turning in herself.

Show me how to act toward him, she prayed silently as she entered the room. *What to say . . .*

But there was no need. The final football game of the day still filled the screen, but Chet had rolled over, pulled the covers up to his neck, and was either asleep or doing a good job of faking it.

She sighed, thinking of the long months when Chet had been gone, especially on his last deployment. She'd marked the days on the calendar, prayed for him faithfully, and rejoiced when the time finally came for him to come home.

Only this time she felt as if he never had. If anything, living with the growing gap between them was more even difficult than when he'd been in Afghanistan. At least then she'd been able to look forward to his homecoming. Now she wondered if he'd ever really come home again.

BREANNA WAS watching for Jeneen and Kevin. After talking with her husband the day before and his confirmation that it might be nice to get their families together, Breanna decided to initiate the relationship and invite the Masons over for dinner one evening soon.

Her anxious thoughts pulled her eyes from the preschool's front door to the mat beside the far wall where

Ryan played with his favorite blocks. She'd tried moving his mat to the center of the room so he wouldn't be so isolated, but Ryan immediately moved it back against the wall. Obviously he felt better when isolated, but Breanna longed to move him past that point.

She glanced back at the front door and then at her watch. Jeneen and Kevin should be arriving any minute. Breanna knew there were days Jeneen didn't bring Kevin because his dad was home and looked after him instead. But Jeneen had told her during lunch that her husband's job should last at least through this week, meaning that Kevin would be here on those days.

Sure enough, the door opened and Jeneen walked in, holding Kevin's hand. The boy wore a light jacket, perfect for these cool fall mornings. Even as Jeneen bent down to say goodbye to her son, his face lit up when he spotted his two best friends approaching him.

"We were waiting for you," James announced.

"Yeah," Mark added. "Let's go play on the slide."

Kevin's face nearly glowed, as he squirmed to get loose from his mother's grip.

"Just one minute, young man," she said, kneeling at eye level with him now. "I need a big hug and kiss before you go play."

The child looked torn but quickly threw his arms around his mother and gave her a kiss. "Bye, Mom," he called, already pulling away to join his friends.

Jeneen stood just as Breanna approached. "Hey, Jeneen," she called out. "Got a minute?"

Jeneen's eyebrows shot up, and she shrugged. "Sure. What's up?"

An excited squeal from the other side of the room caught Breanna's attention, but she saw that Dani was on her way to check on the situation, so she turned her attention back to Jeneen. "It was so nice sharing lunch with you yesterday—even if it was fast food." She laughed, and Jeneen chuckled and nodded. "I just wish your husband could have joined us."

Jeneen's cheeks flushed, and Breanna wondered if she'd stepped on a sensitive area. She decided not to pursue it.

"Actually, Steve and I were talking about it yesterday afternoon, and we thought it might be nice if we got together sometime—you know, us girls, our sons, and of course, our hubbies." She smiled. "I know you said Chet's a former Marine, right? Steve did three years in the Army, including some time in the Middle East, so they should hit it off just fine."

"Oh." Jeneen's mouth formed a circle as she spoke, and once again Breanna wondered if she was treading where she shouldn't.

Breanna shrugged, as if to make light of it. "Not a big deal, really, but we thought . . . well, maybe you could all come over for dinner sometime." When Jeneen still didn't answer, Breanna decided to turn the attention elsewhere. "I'm sure you've noticed that Ryan doesn't socialize well." She let her eyes flit to the mat by the wall. He was still there. "Anyway," she said, clearing her throat before continuing, "I hoped he and Kevin might get to know each other if we all spent time together. Kevin is so friendly and outgoing, and I think Ryan might respond to that."

"I . . . I noticed Ryan is a bit bashful," Jeneen spoke. She offered a weak smile. "I'm sure Kevin would love to spend time with him. But I . . ." Her voice trailed off, and she cleared her throat again. "I'm not sure about my husband. His . . . work schedule fluctuates quite a bit. I'd have to . . . ask him."

"Of course." Breanna smiled. "No rush. Just thought I'd mention it. Consider it an open invitation."

"I will." Jeneen's smile widened slightly. "Thanks, but . . . I need to get going. Don't want to be late for work."

Breanna watched her exit the building. With a sigh and a shake of her head, she turned and went to check on the children who were coloring at a nearby table.

CHAPTER 7

*J*eneen hated starting the day off feeling tired and cranky. She owed it to her boss as well as her customers to show an upbeat and enthusiastic attitude, but right now that was going to take some serious effort.

She hung her jacket in the employee closet in the break room, ignored the coffee pot, and headed straight for her teller window. She stuck her purse in the cupboard underneath the top drawer then went to the vault to pick up her cash drawer.

Once she was ready to open, she locked her cash drawer and checked her watch. *Fifteen minutes until we open. Perfect. Just enough time for a quick cup of coffee.*

She nodded at the other employees who, like her, had come to the break room to grab a last cup before the doors opened for the day. Mondays were always busier than usual, especially in the morning when the merchants came in with weekend deposits. Breaks would be hard to come by.

Jeneen poured her coffee. She really didn't mind being busy. In fact, today she preferred it to thinking about the situation at home. Chet had gotten up and showered and headed to work before she or Kevin even woke up. Apparently he wanted it that way.

"Where's Daddy?" Kevin had asked when he rolled out of bed and headed straight for his parents' room, only to find Jeneen making the bed. "Is he in the kitchen?"

Jeneen's heart constricted. The little boy with the tousled blond curls and still dressed in his action-figure pajamas rubbed his eyes as he awaited her answer.

She smiled and laid a hand on top of his head. "He's already at work," she said. "I guess he had to go in early."

The edges of the child's mouth drooped. "I thought he was going to keep me today while you were at work."

Jeneen shook her head. "Afraid not, sweetheart. Not until this job of his is finished. Then Daddy will stay home with you. But today you get to go back to preschool and see your friends."

His smile and dancing eyes were back. "James and Mark? And we can play on the slide?"

"You sure can." She chuckled. "But first, breakfast. What are you hungry for?"

"Bacon!"

She sighed and shook her head. "You sure are the bacon boy, aren't you? All right, let's go find the bacon Daddy fixed yesterday. We can warm it up, and I'll fix you some pancakes to go with it."

"Yay!"

Kevin had raced for the kitchen, with Jeneen following.

Please, Lord, she prayed now as she rinsed her cup in the sink and then headed back to her station. *Please help us find our way back together again. I miss my husband . . .*

CHET FELT terrible. He had come to the jobsite early and thrown himself into his work, but he couldn't escape his guilt at having treated Jeneen so badly.

She doesn't deserve it, he reminded himself. *She's a good wife and mother, and now she's stuck working fulltime besides. On top of that, I don't go to church with her, and then I get upset when she stops for lunch with friends after the service. How was she supposed to know I'd decided to cook something? It's not like I do it regularly or anything—not even on days when she's working and I'm not.*

A soulful country-and-western song about lost love drifted his way. One of his coworkers had brought a radio, no doubt. He couldn't understand how anybody could listen to that stuff. If he wasn't already depressed before he heard it, he would be by the time a couple of songs had sawed away at his heart.

What's wrong with me? Why can't I let Jeneen back in, the way it was before...? He shook his head and grabbed another handful of finishing nails, shirt-pocketing all but one of them for easy access. He knew it wasn't Jeneen's fault—none of it. It was all his, all part of his readjustment to civilian life. But why was it so hard? He'd known plenty of people who'd transitioned out of the military with little or no problem. Why couldn't he do the same?

A flash of light exploded in his mind then vanished as quickly as it came. He didn't even realize his hands were shaking until he tried to hammer the tiny finishing nail and slammed his thumb instead.

"Ouch!" A couple of swear words followed before he could clamp his mouth shut. The last thing he wanted was to draw attention to himself. He needed this job for as long as it lasted, and he sure didn't want anyone noticing how shaky he was at that moment.

Slow, deep breaths. You can do it, man.

His heart rate returned to normal and he went back to work, determined not to let his mind wander again.

JENEEN AND Kevin stopped at the store on the way to buy a couple of things for dinner. By the time they got home, Chet was pulling into the garage just ahead of them.

Jeneen took a deep breath. Oh, how she prayed this night would go better than the day before.

"Daddy!" Kevin was calling for Chet and waving his drawing before any of them climbed out of their vehicles. "Want to see what I made at school today?"

Chet got to the car before Jeneen had time to get Kevin out. "I'll get him," he said, shooting a brief smile her way.

A tiny ray of hope penetrated what felt like the cold, hard darkness of her heart.

"Please, God," she whispered under her breath.

The three of them made their way into the house, with Kevin riding on his dad's shoulders and chattering the entire time. Jeneen was encouraged that Chet seemed to be paying attention. He had even grabbed the bag of groceries from her car and carried it inside.

"I'm going to get dinner started," she announced, trying to keep her tone nonchalant. "Shouldn't take more than half an hour or so."

Chet, with Kevin's head resting on top of his and the boy's legs dangling over the front of his shoulders, turned to her. "We'll go wash up," he said, his voice softer than it had been since the fiasco of the day before. "Then we'll come back and set the table." He smiled again, broader this time, and then twisted his head to peer upward at Kevin. "Isn't that right, buddy? You and I can handle that, can't we?"

Kevin enthusiastically agreed, and the two of them headed down the hallway toward the bathroom, leaving Jeneen to fight tears of relief as she unpacked the groceries.

CHAPTER 8

The remainder of the week passed uneventfully, and Jeneen was grateful. She was getting better at balancing her job and all the things that needed to be managed at home, but throw a moody husband into the mix and it was just too much.

She glanced in the rearview mirror and saw that Kevin had nodded off. No surprise there, as Breanna had warned her that the three-year-old hadn't had much of a nap that day.

The rest of her conversation with Breanna Pritchard replayed in her mind. From the beginning Jeneen had taken to the woman who owned and operated Sunny Days Preschool and Daycare. Jeneen liked the woman's outgoing, down-to-earth personality, and since Jeneen and Kevin had run into Breanna and her family at the fast-food restaurant after church the previous week, Jeneen knew she was right to have suspected Breanna shared her Christian faith.

But now Breanna had extended an invitation for Jeneen and Chet and Kevin to come to their house for dinner Sunday afternoon—"after church." Jeneen hit her left-turn signal and turned onto the street where she lived. With her house in sight, she wondered how Chet would react to the invitation. He'd always been so friendly and outgoing, making friends easily. Since coming home from his last deployment, however, that hadn't been the case. He hadn't seemed interested in visiting his pre-military friends, and he'd done nothing to stay in touch with the other men in his unit. How would he feel about visiting people he didn't know at all, particularly when those people were Christians?

She hit the garage door opener and pulled inside. *Please, Lord,* she prayed silently, glancing at Chet's truck already in its parking place, *let him be willing to at least give it a try. It would be so nice to have a social life again.* She thought then how she should have warned Breanna that Chet wasn't a believer, but maybe she'd have a chance to work it into the conversation when she called Breanna to accept or decline the invitation.

Taking a deep breath, she stepped out of the car and went to get her still-sleeping son from the backseat.

CHET STOOD at the stove, stirring macaroni into the boiling water when Jeneen came in, carrying Kevin. He set down the spoon and took their sleeping son from his mother's arms. Leaning down just enough to give Jeneen a quick peck on the lips, he then whispered, "Do you want him to keep sleeping, or should I wake him up?"

His wife's grateful smile warmed his heart. "Let's let him sleep a few more minutes, at least until supper's ready."

He nodded and took Kevin to his room, where he laid him gently on the bed. When he got back to the kitchen, Jeneen had picked up where he left off, stirring the macaroni and flipping the turkey burgers.

"Hey," he said, coming up behind her and slipping his arms around her waist. "I can finish that."

She gave a slight shake of her head. "That's all right. It looks like you've got everything under control. I'll just keep an eye on what's on the stove if you want to make a salad and set the table."

He kissed her neck, resisting the urge to nuzzle into her warmth and pull her close. But the meal needed to be completed, so he let her go. "Sure. Glad to do it."

He watched her from the corner of his eye as he washed and prepared the vegetables for a salad. Then he set the table, wondering why her back seemed a bit stiff and she was quieter than usual. Was she upset with him in some way?

Chet sighed and shook his head. He had to stop being so negative. She was probably just tired. It was Friday evening, after all, and she'd put in a long week. So had he, of course, but—

"Honey, can you grab the butter and milk from the fridge?"

"Sure," he said, opening the refrigerator. "Here you go."

She smiled up at him, but the smile didn't extend to her eyes. He knew her well enough to be sure then that something was on her mind. Should he ask her now, or wait until later?

Before he could turn away, she laid her hand on his arm and smiled up at him. "Um . . . can I ask you something?"

There it was.

He shrugged. "Sure. What's up?"

A flicker of doubt crossed her face before her smile returned. "I think I've mentioned the lady who runs Kevin's preschool, right? Breanna Pritchard?"

The name didn't ring a bell, but Chet was relatively certain that Jeneen must have at least mentioned her at some point, so he nodded. "Sure. What about her?"

Jeneen dropped her eyes, as if it took all her concentration to check the pasta. "She . . . invited us to come to dinner on Sunday."

Us? As in you and Kevin, or us, as in all three of us? He felt his shoulders tense as he realized he already knew the answer to that one. "Why would she do that?" he asked, turning away to finish setting the table. "I mean, is that something she does with all the parents, or are we special in some way?"

His wife's hesitation caused his tension to move from his shoulders to his jaw, but he wasn't going to say another word until she did.

"Well, no, not really. She doesn't do this with all the parents, so I guess we are special in a way." Jeneen turned to face him, and his gut clenched. He wasn't going to like this.

"Breanna and her husband have a son about Kevin's age. He's . . . adopted. We thought it might be nice for all of us to get together and let the boys get acquainted."

Chet frowned. "I don't get it. Isn't her son at the preschool? Why can't they get to know each other there?"

Her cheeks flushed slightly before she replied. "Her son isn't very . . . sociable. He has a hard time making friends and pretty much just keeps to himself."

Chet related to the boy without even meeting him, but he wasn't about to say so. He continued to wait.

"Anyway," Jeneen said, "we thought it would be nice for all of us to get together after church and see how the boys do when there aren't other children around to distract them."

"After church?" Chet's jaw clenched again. "So these people go to our church too?"

She shook her head. "Oh, no. They go to another one, but we ran into each other last Sunday and had lunch together. That's when we discovered we were all on our way home from church."

All? Not all. I wasn't there. "So what did they say about me not going to church with you? They must have thought that was pretty strange."

"Oh, no, not at all!" Her answer came too quickly. "They didn't even think about it, I'm sure. It . . . it never even came up."

"Right." He went to the refrigerator to retrieve the salad dressing. He sensed her come up behind him.

"Really, Chet," she said, a hint of pleading in her voice. "They didn't say anything about it at all. And they wouldn't. They just invited us for dinner, that's all."

He turned to face her. "They invited us for dinner on Sunday—after church. You don't think the topic's going to come up?" He nudged her aside and went to place the bottle of dressing on the table.

"Chet, please . . ."

"Why can't you just leave it alone?" Refusing to turn back to face her, he continued. "Don't think I don't know what you're doing, Jeneen. You're always trying to get me to come to church with you or to meet your religious friends. I'm not interested, OK? So no to the Sunday dinner thing."

He clenched his jaw one last time. "It's time to eat. I'm going to get Kevin up." He headed for the hallway, calling back over his shoulder, "If you and Kevin want to go, feel free. And while you're there, let her know that Kevin won't be in school for a while. He'll be staying with me until I can find another job. The one I had ended today."

WHEN AM *I going to learn about timing?* she thought as she cleared the table after a relatively quiet meal. Kevin had still been sleepy, so his usual chatter was somewhat subdued, and she and Chet had spoken only in response to Kevin's limited dialogue. Now Chet was giving Kevin his bath while she cleaned up the kitchen, fighting hot tears that stung her eyelids.

I should have waited until he'd had a chance to tell me about his job ending. We expected it would be soon, but I know how hard he takes it when I'm working and he's not. She sighed and rinsed the silverware before placing it in the dishwasher. *The two things that seem to bother him most are when he's not working and when he thinks I'm pushing my "religion" on him—even though I'm not. So tonight he had both those things hit him at the same time.* She closed her eyes. *What now, Lord? How do I handle this?* A sense of reassurance flowed over her like warm honey, and she smiled in spite of her concerns. *Thank You, Lord. Knowing You're with us is enough. We'll get through this. . . .*

She finished cleaning up the kitchen and then went to join her family, determined not to mention the invitation again. She'd call Breanna the next day and let her know they couldn't make it.

CHAPTER 9

Once Kevin was down for the night, Jeneen had hoped to smooth things over with Chet, but he had gone straight to their room and turned on the TV. By the time she climbed in beside him, he was lying on his side with his back to her. She was certain he wasn't asleep, but his do-not-disturb message was loud and clear. So she'd turned off the TV and eventually drifted off to sleep.

When she awoke the next morning, Chet's side of the bed was empty. He wasn't in the kitchen having coffee, and when she opened the door to check the garage, she saw that his truck was gone.

Once again blinking back hot tears, she made a pot of coffee and sat down to read her Bible and pray before Kevin woke up. She was nursing her second cup and underlining as she read through Matthew 6, taking comfort in the familiar verses, when Kevin shuffled in, his blond curls in disarray and his eyes still heavy with sleep.

"Where's Daddy?"

She held out her arms, and he climbed up on her lap. Even with Chet having been gone for so many months, it hadn't taken Kevin long to adapt to having him home again. Jeneen was pleased that the two "men" in her life had re-bonded so quickly. If only she and Chet could do the same.

"Daddy will be home soon," she said. "He probably just went to the store for something."

"Maybe he's working," Kevin suggested, his head leaning against Jeneen's chest.

She kissed the top of his head. "No, sweetheart, he's not working today. In fact, Daddy finished his job, and now he'll be staying home with you until he finds another one."

Kevin lifted his head, his blue eyes serious. "But what about James and Mark? They want to play with me at school."

Jeneen was surprised. This was not a reaction she expected. Kevin seemed to like school, and she knew he enjoyed playing with his friends, but she'd assumed he preferred spending time with his dad to just about anything else. "Don't you want to stay with Daddy?"

Kevin nodded. "I want to stay with Daddy, but I want to play with my friends too."

Jeneen sighed and offered a solution. "Tell you what. Until Daddy finds a new job, you can stay with him most of the time but still go to school at least one day a week. What do you think about that?"

Kevin's face lit up, and he nodded. "I like that. James and Mark will like it too."

She smiled and kissed his forehead. "I'm sure they will."

The sound of the garage door opening caught their attention, and Kevin hopped down from her lap. "Daddy's home!" He raced to the door and opened it, standing there in his superhero pajamas as he waited for Chet.

He didn't have long to wait. With scarcely a nod of recognition to Jeneen, Chet had come in and laid a bag of donuts on the table. Then he'd lifted his son onto his shoulders before heading down the hallway. "We'll come back and have donuts after we play a while, OK, son?"

Jeneen sighed again. Donuts. They all loved them, but she couldn't help but feel a tinge of guilt when she or Chet splurged on unnecessary treats. Besides, it was obvious things hadn't gotten any better between herself and her husband during the night.

She glanced at her watch. Eight o'clock. She'd give it another hour and then call Breanna to decline her invitation for Sunday.

ONCE AGAIN, Chet realized he was being a jerk, and he hated himself for it. But he didn't seem able to push past it and go apologize, even though he knew he should. Instead, he hid himself in his son's room, pretending there was nothing he'd rather do than play Matchbox cars with a three-year-old.

His mind flashed to the open Bible on the table in front of Jeneen when he'd come home from his early-morning ride. If she'd just lay off the church stuff, he could put up with the rest—at least, he hoped he could. He'd been fighting depression when he got the last check on Friday and knew for certain the job had ended. Sure, he'd expected it, but he kept hoping—

"Daddy, look!"

His son's voice interrupted what he sensed was a real pity-party coming on. "Hey, that's great," he said, watching Kevin roll his two favorite vehicles from the edge of the bed onto the floor below. It didn't take much to please his son, and Chet appreciated that. Maybe that was the reason he could still connect with Kevin. If only Jeneen were so easy to please.

To be fair, she never complained about having to go back to work, even though they both knew the only reason she did was because he was no longer supporting his family. He'd really messed up by not staying in the Marines, but he hadn't been able to accept the possibility of going back to the Middle East again. Even now the memories snuck up on him and tried to smother him at the most unexpected times. It took all the strength and concentration he could muster to keep them at bay.

A stab of guilt twisted his heart. In all honesty, Jeneen hadn't mentioned going to church. She'd simply included him in an invitation to go to dinner at his son's preschool director's home. There was a time that would have seemed a simple and reasonable request. He couldn't deny it was still reasonable, but it certainly wasn't simple. He didn't like meeting new people, especially church people, who had such different standards. It meant he'd have to be on his best behavior the entire time he was there. One slip-up and they'd spot him for the phony he was. Why couldn't Jeneen understand that and not put him in such an awkward position?

Memories of how desperately he had missed his wife while he was in Afghanistan haunted him now. His wish had come true; he had returned safe and sound to his family, even though others hadn't. He blinked away the flash of light, refusing to acknowledge the specifics of the losses he'd experienced. The important thing was that he was home now, with his wife and son. Isn't that what he'd wanted the entire time he was gone? So why wasn't it enough now?

"I'll be right back, buddy," Chet said, tousling Kevin's hair. "Hold my spot for me, will you?"

Kevin nodded. "Hurry!"

Chet smiled as he stood to his feet. "I will, son."

JENEEN WAS making the bed when Chet entered their cramped but cozy room.

"Hey," he said.

She forced a smile. "Hey, yourself. Thanks for the donuts."

He nodded. "I know it's not a very healthy breakfast, but it's Saturday, you know."

It was her turn to nod. "I know."

"I'll make some fresh orange juice," Chet offered, his smile weak. "That'll help offset all that sugar a little."

He was trying to bridge the gap, and her heart leapt to meet him halfway, more if necessary. She stopped fluffing pillows and walked up to him. "I'm sorry," she said. "I didn't mean to put you in an awkward position. I'll call in a little while and tell them we can't come."

Chet shook his head. "Don't. I've got to stop being so defensive. I'll go." He pulled her into his arms. "But let's don't stay too long, OK?"

She laid her head against his chest. With his heart beating in her ear, she nodded. "Of course. We won't stay long at all." She tightened her arms around him. "And thank you."

CHAPTER 10

*J*eneen woke up Sunday morning with a sense of unease hanging over her. What was wrong? Why did she feel such apprehension?

She glanced at the other side of the bed where her husband still slept. Ah, now she remembered. Chet had come around and told her to accept the invitation for dinner today, so long as she kept their visit short. She'd agreed and told Breanna they'd be coming for dinner but not immediately after church as they had other plans. Jeneen had offered no specific reason, as she really didn't want to lie to her new friend.

Breanna had graciously accepted Jeneen's explanation, and when Jeneen asked what she could bring, Breanna had suggested dessert. "Whatever you three want to have is fine with us," she'd said with a chuckle. "You'd be hard-pressed to find a dessert we don't like."

And so Jeneen had planned to get up early and make a batch of chocolate cupcakes, which she'd frost after church this afternoon. She couldn't imagine anyone—particularly three-year-old boys—not liking chocolate cupcakes.

She glanced at the digital clock at her bedside. Six-thirty. Hmm, she could actually stay in bed for another half-hour or so and still be done in plenty of time to take Kevin to church and Sunday school. Then again, she was already awake, so . . .

She pulled herself from bed and headed for the bathroom. There was nothing like a good hot shower to get her moving in the morning. She hummed a soft version of "O Come All Ye Faithful" as she stepped into the shower and let the warm spray cascade over her. It might be a little early for Christmas carols since they were still a few weeks away from Thanksgiving, but "O Come All Ye Faithful" was the song that had danced around the edges of her thoughts since awakening that morning.

BREANNA HAD overslept and was now rushing around to try to pull everything—and everybody—together in time to head for church. Steve would take care of himself, as he always did, but their son was another story.

"Ryan, I told you, you have to get up and get dressed. It's almost time to leave for church."

She'd come into his room thirty minutes earlier to wake him, as she knew he wasn't one to get going quickly in the morning. But now she'd had her shower and come back to find Ryan still in bed, the clothes she'd laid out for him still at the foot of his bed where she'd left them.

Breanna sighed. She adored this child, but he was most certainly a challenge.

"Ryan, come on, let's go." She pulled the covers back, and there he lay—curled up in his pajamas, unmoving, his eyes scrunched shut.

She sat down on the side of his bed and leaned over, slipping her arms under his shoulders in a hug and nuzzling the warmth of his soft neck. "Come on, big boy. I know you're awake, and it's time to get going. Mommy slept late, but we still have time for your favorite cereal if you get up right now."

He rewarded her with one open brown eye. "Honey-Nut Cheerios?"

Breanna smiled and nodded. "Absolutely. But you have to get up now, or we'll be late."

He closed his eye again, and she watched him wrestle with the temptation. She kissed his cheek, shooting up a silent prayer. *Please, Father, help him to adapt to church and to enjoy going there so we won't have this problem every Sunday morning.*

Then she thought of how they enacted similar scenes almost every morning of his life, whether it entailed going to preschool or to the grocery store. It was as if he considered his bed a safe spot and didn't want to leave.

At last she picked him up and carried him to the chair near the end of his bed. She sat down with Ryan in her lap and began to pull off his pajama top. "You're such a big boy now, it sure would be nice if you helped me with this." The top came off, and Breanna laid it on the bed.

She looked back at her son. Both eyes were open now, and he was studying her. Oh, how she wished she could crawl inside that mind of his and find out what he was thinking! Then again, maybe she wouldn't like it so much.

"Did you have a good sleep?"

With his dark hair sticking out in wisps and tangles, he nodded.

She smiled. At least it was something.

"That's good," she said, removing him from her lap and standing him up in front of her so she could help him step out of his pajama pants. He'd had his bath last night before going to bed, so all she needed to do now was get him to wash his face, brush his teeth and comb his hair. Sliding him into his church clothes would be a snap after all that.

She glanced at her watch. Uh oh. If she was going to have time to get a bowl of cereal down this nearly statue-still three-year-old, they were going to have to hustle.

Breanna smiled at him. "I have a surprise for you, Ryan. You're going to love it."

Was that a flash of interest she saw dart through his brown eyes? Encouraged, she said, "You remember Kevin from school? He's the new boy who plays on the slide a lot. We had lunch with him and his mom after church last week."

No reaction, no response.

She sighed. "After church, today we're going to come home, and after lunch and a nap, you can help me fix dinner because Kevin and his mommy and daddy are coming to visit us. You can take Kevin to your room and play together. Won't that be fun?"

Ryan's eyes hooded nearly shut, and he lowered his gaze to the floor. Then he leaned into Breanna and let her hold him close—a privilege that he doled out quite sparingly.

"What is it, sweetheart?" she asked, stroking his hair and reveling in his intimate gesture. "Are you happy that Kevin's coming to visit? Is that it?"

His face still buried against her chest, he shook his head no, and a sob hiccupped from deep inside him, bringing a rush of hot tears to Breanna's eyes. Was there no way to reach this beloved, wounded child? She and Steve had tried nearly everything to entice him out of his protective shell and into at least a few social situations. But so far they'd batted zero. Ryan seemed to have adapted to living with them, but he also seemed unwilling to move beyond the four walls of their home.

And so she'd opted to invite a potential playmate to come here, which was familiar territory for Ryan. Surely he'd come around after Kevin and his parents had been here for a while . . . wouldn't he?

She smiled and pried him away from her chest. "Come on, sweetheart. We don't have much time. Let's finish getting you dressed and ready for church. You want to have enough time for your cereal, don't you?"

Ryan didn't answer, though he passively responded to her instructions until they were ready to head to the kitchen for a quick breakfast.

JENEEN HAD a hard time concentrating on the sermon that morning. Her mind kept drifting to their evening plans and wondering how Chet would behave.

Unbelievable, she thought, standing for the closing hymn. *I should be worrying about how my three-year-old will behave at someone else's home, but instead I'm worrying about my husband.*

She sighed and pushed the thoughts from her mind, concentrating instead on reading and singing the words on the screen in front. Then the pastor pronounced the benediction and sent them on their way, though not without first inviting anyone who needed prayer to come up front, where he and two of the elders would be waiting.

Jeneen seriously considered going up and asking for prayer about the situation with Chet. It wasn't just how he might behave or react this evening, but rather his behavior in general. At times she caught brief glimpses of the kind, considerate man she'd married, but those glimpses were coming less often with each passing day. But there was no time to linger today; she needed to pick up her son and get home.

Standing at the open doorway of the three-to-five-year old class, she waved at Kevin to get his attention. He smiled and jumped up from the small group of boys where he'd been working on a huge Lego project. She picked up the pen on the nearby desk and signed him out of class.

"Mom, can we stay a little longer?"

Jeneen set down the pen and raised her eyebrows at her son. "No, honey, we can't. Did you forget we're going to Ryan's for dinner tonight?"

His pleading look only grew more pitiful. "But that's not until later. Can't we just stay here for a little while? We're not done building yet."

The teacher, Melissa Greggs, stepped up and intervened at that moment, laying a hand on top of Kevin's shoulder. "Kevin, I'm sure the Legos will be here waiting for you when you come next week. But your mom's here now, and you need to get your things and go with her." She pointed to one of three small round tables and said, "Your Bible and papers are right there. You don't want to forget those. You'll need them for next week's lesson."

Kevin's shoulders drooped, and he nodded before turning to trudge over to the table and pick up his things. He was still dragging his feet when he returned to the doorway.

"Tell Miss Greggs goodbye," Jeneen said.

Without looking up, he murmured, "Goodbye, Miss Greggs."

Jeneen smiled and nodded her own goodbye to the teacher then took her son's free hand. "Come on, sweetheart. Daddy's waiting for us, and we have to frost those cupcakes."

Kevin's head shot up, and the excitement returned to his face. "Cupcakes! I forgot."

He began to surge ahead, pulling on Jeneen's hand. "Come on, Mom. Let's go!"

Jeneen chuckled and shook her head. It was amazing how quickly a child's mood could change. *Almost as quickly as Chet's,* she thought, picking up her pace just a bit as they headed for their car.

CHAPTER 11

The cupcakes were perfect—light, fluffy, and moist. Now all they needed to do was frost them.

Chet had gone into the family room after lunch to watch a football game, and the last time Jeneen had checked on him, he was snoozing in his favorite chair. Kevin had taken a short nap, giving her a chance to put her feet up as well. But her son was awake now and anxious to get started.

"Come on, Mom," he said, holding her hand in both of his as he gently tugged. "You said I could help you frost the cupcakes after my nap." He grinned, his blue eyes dancing under his unruly blond curls. "I took my nap, and so did you. Let's go!"

Unable to resist, Jeneen returned his smile. As much as she might like a few more minutes of quiet, it was obvious she wasn't going to get it—not today anyway. "OK, you're right. Naptime is over."

Kevin's blond curls bounced as he nodded his head. "And you can help me lick the beaters and the bowl when we're done."

Jeneen laughed. How could she turn down an offer like that?

She pulled herself from the bed and followed Kevin down the hallway toward the kitchen. On the way by the family room, she peeked in to check on Chet. Still sleeping in front of the TV. He hadn't said much before or after Jeneen and Kevin went to church, but she knew he was thinking about dinner tonight.

Jeneen already enjoyed Breanna, just from the little they'd talked. So as far as she was concerned, their relationship could only get better. And Kevin was so outgoing that she had no problem imagining him becoming quick friends with Breanna's son, Ryan—though that would depend a lot on Ryan's response.

She glanced at Kevin, who was pulling the stool up to the counter where the cupcakes waited in their colorful paper dressings. His eyes sparkled with anticipation, and she smiled to think how he would no doubt bring Ryan out of his shell in record time.

I've always thought Kevin was one of the friendliest, most cheerful people on earth. I don't think he's ever not taken to someone, so I'm sure today won't be an exception.

She sighed as she grabbed the mixing bowl and set it on the counter, then pulled milk and butter from the fridge and rummaged in the cupboard until she found the powdered sugar and unsweetened cocoa. *I just wish Chet could be a little more like Kevin. He's never been a major extrovert, but since he got home this last time, it seems like he's turning into some sort of recluse.*

She shook her head. No sense worrying about something that might not happen—particularly when she could pray about it and leave it in God's hands.

As she tied an apron on her excited son, she did her best to turn the entire situation over to God—and to leave it there. After all, she certainly couldn't fix it herself . . .

"Here, honey, let me help you with that."

Steve's offer was so typical of him, and Breanna smiled up at him. "You are the best husband ever. Did you know that?"

He laughed. "Absolutely. And don't you ever forget it. Besides, work's more fun when you share it with somebody."

Breanna stifled the temptation to remind him of his one imperfection—sloppiness. She was forever picking up his socks or helping him find his keys. But in light of his many positive qualities, she let it go.

She thought then how nice it would be if she could somehow get Ryan involved in helping to get ready for their company that evening. Even a three-year-old could help set a table or . . . something. She sighed. She had to face facts. Ryan wasn't like most three-year-olds. The social worker had told them he'd likely never be like most kids, but they'd hoped . . . and prayed, as they continued to do daily.

Now she nodded at her husband as they finished setting the table. He was right. Work was more enjoyable when you shared it with someone. She might never get Ryan out here to join in, but she really did have the very best husband ever.

As they headed back into the kitchen to check on the spaghetti sauce, she asked, "Do you think I should have fixed something else? Not everyone likes spaghetti."

Steve chuckled and shook his head. "Listen, beautiful lady, some people might not like regular old spaghetti sauce, but nobody in their right mind wouldn't love yours." His dark eyes shone, contrasting with his caramel-colored skin, and he pulled her into his arms. He was tall enough that Breanna could lean against his chest and listen to his steady heartbeat. It was a familiar sound that had brought security and peace to her life many times during their seven years of marriage.

She smiled at the memory of their wedding. Her mother had taken to Steve immediately, but her father had held out before warming up to him. Steve had been so sure it was because he was African American, but Breanna knew better. Her father would have been suspicious of anyone who'd been out to woo his baby girl away, and Steve was no exception.

But eventually the families on both sides had made peace with the situation and had been thrilled when the couple adopted the tiny Mexican-American boy named Ryan. The child's too-big eyes were soulful and seemed to win everyone over the minute he looked at them. But the feeling wasn't mutual. He had come to live with Steve and Breanna just before his second birthday. But no matter how hard his grandparents or aunts or uncles or cousins tried to bond with him, the little boy who'd been rescued from a drug house after his mother died of an overdose seemed determined to not let anyone else in.

Pulling herself away from her husband's chest and lifting her head to look into his kind face, she voiced her concerns about the day. "It's not just the spaghetti sauce."

Steve nodded. "I know. You're worried about Ryan."

Hot tears pricked her eyes. "You know how he is around people. He still hasn't made any friends at preschool. But I just thought . . . well, maybe if a little boy about his age came over, and it was just . . . the two of them . . ."

Her voice trailed off, and she realized she didn't have to finish her sentence. Steve knew exactly what she was thinking.

He kissed her forehead. "Come on. Let's get that sauce stirred before it burns. And I guarantee you—these people are going to love your spaghetti. And as for Ryan . . ." He pulled her close again. "Our son is in the Father's hands, and there's no better place for him to be than that."

CHET'S STOMACH was in knots by the time they arrived at the Pritchards' home. What had he been thinking to agree to this invitation? He didn't know these people, hadn't even met them, and now he was going to be stuck with them for an entire evening.

Not only that, he thought, as they stood on the porch, waiting to be let in, *they're religious people, just like Jeneen, so I'll probably have to put up with their Bible-talk for the next few hours—especially when they find out I'm not a part of their faith.*

The door opened then, and a petite woman with short red curls and very green eyes flashed them a dazzling smile. "Welcome!" she said, as a tall African-American man walked up and stood behind her. "We're so glad you're here."

The couple opened the door a bit farther and stepped back to give their company plenty of room to enter. They went through the obligatory greetings and introductions, with Chet doing his best to keep his smile in place, though he would have given just about anything to be anywhere else at that moment.

"Where's Ryan?" Kevin asked, looking around. "We brought cupcakes."

Breanna's face flushed pink, but she maintained her happy appearance. "He's in his room," she said then looked toward her husband. "Honey, why don't you take Kevin to Ryan's room?" She smiled down at Kevin. "I'm sure he'll be pleased to hear you brought cupcakes."

Kevin nodded. "Everybody loves cupcakes," he announced then followed Ryan's dad down the hall.

"Come on into the family room," Breanna said, leading the way. "Dinner will be ready soon." She glanced back at them. "I hope you like spaghetti. It's sort of my specialty."

"We love spaghetti," Jeneen said, taking in her husband with a raised eyebrow. "Don't we, honey?"

Chet cleared his throat and forced a smile. "Um, yeah, sure. Who doesn't like spaghetti?"

Breanna laughed. "Like, who doesn't like cupcakes, right?"

They all chuckled as they settled onto the two couches that adjoined at the room's corner. Chet was wondering how much he'd be required to contribute to the conversation when Steve came back into the room.

"Did you get the boys introduced and playing together?" Breanna asked.

Steve raised his eyebrows and nodded. "They're introduced anyway. Not sure how quickly they'll start playing together."

Breanna's checks flushed again, and she clutched her hands together. "Ryan is . . . well, a bit bashful." She exchanged a quick glance with her husband. "I assume you know he's adopted, right?"

No, Chet had not known that, but he really didn't see that it was relevant.

"I wasn't completely certain about that," Jeneen said, "but I assumed that might be the case when I saw . . . well . . ." Her cheeks were also flushed as she directed her words toward Breanna.

"Yes," Breanna said, her smile widening, "we're quite the rainbow family around here." Her smile faded a bit. "We've been married seven years now and never had any children of our own. When we had the opportunity to adopt Ryan, it seemed like an answer to prayer."

Oh boy, here we go, Chet thought. *It sure didn't take 'em long to get on the God thing.*

"He was such a precious, fragile little boy when we brought him home," Breanna said. "Not quite two years old and already endured more than any child should ever have to." She sighed, and it seemed to Chet that her words had dried up. Then her husband jumped in to fill the void.

"He was rescued from a drug house. His mom died of an overdose, and there weren't any family members to step in and take him." He shook his head. "Hard to believe what some kids have to go through."

Chet couldn't argue with that. He'd seen kids in the Middle East who had lost everything, including family and homes, and had taken to living on the street and begging. Some were even recruited as suicide bombers.

He pushed the thought away and tried to pick up the conversation now that Breanna was speaking again.

"Poor little guy," she said, her green eyes shining with what Chet imagined were tears. "He still hasn't caught up in size for his age, but our biggest challenge is get him to let the walls down. You know what I mean?"

Oh yeah, Chet knew. But he wasn't about to say so.

"We're just hoping we can get him to open up a bit with Kevin—you know, someone his own age," Breanna said.

Jeneen smiled. "Well, if anyone can make that happen, it's Kevin. He can be a chatterbox at times, but he's really friendly and easy-going. I'm sure they'll be friends in no time."

"I hope you're right," Breanna said.

The silence hung heavy for a moment then—until Steve glanced over at Chet and asked, "So, Chet, what do you do?"

This is what I dread the most, he thought. *Worse even than the God stuff. How do I tell him I'm basically a house-husband? That my wife supports us because I can't find a job?*

He forced another tight smile. Might as well get it over with. "Lately I've been working construction," he said, his voice more strained than he meant it to be. "But that's not very steady, I'm afraid."

"I know what you mean," Steve answered with a nod. "I have several friends in the construction field, and they're always scrambling to find work. But you said 'lately.' What did you do before that?"

From the corner of his eye, Chet saw Jeneen stiffen. If she only knew how much he did *not* want to talk about this. He didn't even try to smile as he answered. "I was in the military—Marines."

Steve's face lit up. "The Marines? No kidding! I was in the Army, but my younger brother's in the Marines right now. Just got back from a deployment to Afghanistan. You ever serve over there?"

"Twice. I don't really like to talk about it."

Steve's face reflected his surprise, but he quickly got it under control. "Can't say that I blame you," he said then looked at Breanna. "So is dinner about ready? If you want to get everyone seated, I'll go get the boys."

Breanna nodded and smiled then stood up to escort them into the dining room. Chet was counting on less talking and more eating during dinner. Then, if all went well, maybe they could escape soon after.

CHAPTER 12

*J*eneen leaned her head back against the front passenger seat as they headed home. She was thankful Chet had insisted on driving, as she was far too exhausted from walking an emotional tightrope all evening. Dinner had been delicious, and Breanna and Steve were a great couple. But Jeneen could hardly keep her eyes off her husband, who sat across from her at the table, sneaking glares at her every so often. It was obvious he wanted nothing more than to finish their meal and get out of there.

Kevin had been great at filling gaps each time the adults went silent. His bubbly personality and friendly, outgoing ways easily complemented all topics of their dinner conversation, even some they would rather have avoided.

"Daddy takes me to the park when he doesn't work."

"Daddy was 'ployed, but now he's back."

"I helped Mommy frost the cupcakes."

"Daddy doesn't like to go to church with us."

Each time their talkative three-year-old piped up with a comment about his daddy, Jeneen saw the flash of irritation on Chet's face. She'd tried more than once to encourage Kevin to stop talking and get back to eating, but Breanna and Steve seemed delighted by his chatter.

They'd scarcely gotten out of the Pritchards' driveway before Kevin fell asleep in his car seat. That's when Jeneen had opted to close her eyes and pretend to be asleep as well. At least it would prolong the confrontation with Chet that she was certain would come once Kevin was in bed.

Why do I even try? Chet doesn't want to socialize, and I need to accept that.

She stifled a yawn, not wanting Chet to realize she was still awake. *It's not like it's just my friends. I've suggested getting together with some of his old buddies, but he nixed that* too. They've even stopped coming by since they figured out he wasn't open to rekindling their relationships. My husband is definitely b coming a hermit. He barely talks to me anymore, and even his relationship with Kevin isn't what it should be. How long until our son senses that and feels rejected? It's one thing for me to experience it, but I couldn't bear to watch Kevin be hurt that way.

She thought then of little Ryan and all he'd been through in his short life, and guilt stabbed her heart. Forgive me, Lord, she prayed silently. We are so blessed to have a healthy, happy child. But Ryan . . .

Jeneen pictured the boy's tiny frame as he sat with them at the table, his head bowed nearly the entire time. He didn't consume half of what Ryan ate, and he didn't contribute to the table conversation at all. The one time she'd caught a glimpse of the child's face, it appeared haunted, sad . . . fearful. And his eyes seemed to live somewhere else.

She had to stop feeling sorry for herself. How dare she when she thought of what so many others went through? A fragile child, helpless, needing loving care and security but receiving just the opposite. It was no wonder he didn't want to chance letting those walls down.

Tomorrow I'm going to ask Kevin what happened when the boys were in Ryan's room. Maybe he opened up a bit there . . . or not.

Without thinking she reached out and laid her hand on Chet's arm. Her sleeping act was busted, but she really needed to connect with him at that moment. If only he felt the same about her. It had been so long since they'd really felt connected, the way they'd been when they first married and when Kevin was born.

All the time, actually, she thought. Up until this last deployment. I just wish I could get him to talk to me about it, to open up a little.

She sighed. That hardly seemed likely, since he scarcely talked to her about anything these days, much less something buried deep inside him.

Tears bit her eyelids at the thought that she just might be losing Chet. She'd prayed him through two deployments, and he'd come home safely both times. Physically, at least. But now he was home, sitting beside her in the car, and she felt as if they were miles apart.

Come back to me, Chet, she begged silently. *Let me into your heart again. I miss you!*

She peered at his profile in the semi-darkness. He hadn't flinched since she laid her hand on his arm. It might have been easier if he'd shaken it off. At least she'd know he was aware of her being there, that he felt her touch him.

Help me, Lord, she prayed. *Show me how to reach him, how to love him as You want me to. I want to be a good wife to Chet, but right now I feel like he doesn't even care if he has one. What happened to him, Father? What nightmares and memories does he wrestle with while he's locked away in his own private world? What can I do to help him? I don't want to lose him, Lord. Please help us. . . .*

"Looks like your spaghetti was a hit," Steve observed as he helped his wife put the last of the plates and utensils into the dishwasher.

Breanna smiled and shrugged. "I think you're right."

"But . . . ?"

She stopped and stared at him, her brows drawn together. "What do you mean, 'but'?"

He grasped her arms and gently pulled her to his chest. "Do you really think I don't know you well enough to know when something's bothering you?"

She sighed, and he felt a tremor pass over her.

"OK, you got me." She pulled back slightly and looked up at him. "The spaghetti was actually the best part of the evening, don't you think? I mean, it was like Chet wanted to be anywhere other than here."

She blinked away tears and dropped her gaze. "And then there's Ryan. I thought for sure he'd open up if he spent time with another boy his age here in familiar territory."

He lifted her chin with his finger. "But he didn't."

She shook her head. "No, he didn't." Tears continued to pool in her green eyes, tugging at his heart. "What are we going to do? I want so much to see him healed of all the pain and rejection he suffered as a baby, but what else can we do that we aren't already doing?"

Steve wiped a tear that had spilled over onto her cheek. "We'll just keep doing what we've been doing. We'll love him unconditionally and try to give him a sense of security—which he's obviously never had." He pulled her against his chest again. "And we'll pray. Every day. Every moment if need be. God loves Ryan more than we do, and we both believe He directed us to adopt him, so we also have to believe that God knows how to reach the little guy. Right?"

He felt her nod against his chest and then relax into his embrace. "Please, Father," he whispered. "Please show us how to love our son in such a way that he no longer fears that we'll hurt or abandon him." Tears stung his own eyes at that moment, and he rested his chin on top of Breanna's head.

WHY COULDN'T she just leave things alone? Why did she have to keep prying and picking—and yes, praying? More than anything else Jeneen did, Chet hated that she continually told him she was praying for him. He couldn't decide if it was because he was insulted that she thought he was so bad he needed all that prayer, or because he figured he was a lost cause and all the prayer in the world wouldn't help. And it was just a matter of time until this conversation started up again tonight.

They'd done OK when they got home from the Pritchards' place. Together they got Kevin ready for bed and tucked in. He even hung around while she and Kevin prayed together. Then he'd escaped to the bedroom to watch some Sunday night football. Regardless of who won the game, it would be the highlight of his day.

He'd closed the door when he came to bed, but now he heard her open it and walk in.

"Who's playing?" she asked, her voice overly animated as if she wanted him to know how much she cared.

"Cowboys and Eagles." He could have told her it was the Elves and the Gremlins, and she wouldn't have known the difference.

She stopped right in front of him, blocking his view. "Who's winning?"

It was obvious her smile was pasted on, but he offered a hint of a smile in return. "It's tied up right now."

"Ah." She nodded and then thankfully moved out of his way and went toward the bathroom. At least he'd have a little bit of a break before she'd joined him under the covers.

He clenched his jaw and ground his teeth. He hated himself when he acted this way, but he just didn't seem able to stop. The minute anyone—particularly Jeneen—said anything negative or critical, he took offense, even though he often knew it wasn't meant that way.

He took a deep breath and tried to refocus on the game, but the screen had just cut to a commercial about new cars. *Ha. I can't even afford to fix the ones we have. At the rate I'm going, we'll probably never be able to drive a new car again.*

In all fairness, he knew he had an exceptional wife who didn't care about such things. She seldom complained about needing anything—clothes, furniture, makeup, whatever. And he couldn't remember the last time she'd said she was going shopping for much of anything besides groceries. When he thought about how many times he'd heard other guys grousing about how much money their wives spent, he felt guiltier than ever.

The bathroom door opened then, and though he tried to keep himself from looking in her direction, he turned his eyes toward her anyway. Big mistake. She stood there with her shoulder-length strawberry blonde hair shining in the overhead light. He didn't even have to get close to her to know how blue her eyes were, which he imagined had something to do with the pair of light blue silk pajamas she had put on.

He quickly tore his gaze away and zeroed back in on the game, which had just resumed. Jeneen was not only reasonable about things like spending, but she was also beautiful. Chet knew he was one lucky guy, but none of that helped right now.

She climbed into bed and snuggled up beside him, nearly bringing tears to his eyes as the smell of her perfume made him lightheaded. How many times had he tried to remember that exact smell when he was overseas, dreaming of the day when he'd finally be home again, right where he was at this minute? More times than he could count, and yet he couldn't bring himself to do something as simple as taking her into his arms and holding her close.

"So what's the score now?" she asked, resting her hand on his chest.

"Still tied."

"Oh." She paused, and he dared to hope she'd be content to lie there and not talk. Of course that didn't happen.

"So what did you think of the Pritchards? Nice people, right?"

"Yeah, right. Nice."

Another pause. "Breanna is really great with the kids at preschool. Kevin really likes her."

"Kevin likes everybody."

He felt her tense a bit, and he knew he'd said something wrong. Seems he couldn't win no matter what he did or said.

"Steve's really nice too," she said, and her body relaxed against him. "Don't you think?"

He nodded, determined not to say the wrong thing.

"I can't help but feel sorry for little Ryan, though. He's just adorable, and Breanna says he's smart as a whip, but . . ."

Her voice trailed off, and he waited, wondering what it was she didn't like about Ryan. Personally, he'd admired the one other person among those sitting around the dining table that evening who hadn't felt the need to chatter incessantly. *Maybe that's why I liked him,* Chet thought. *That little boy is a lot like me.*

Jeneen was still talking—something about Ryan and the other kids at the preschool—and he knew he should pay attention, but he couldn't make himself concentrate. Had he really sunk so low that he didn't care about other people anymore? His wife wasn't asking much. He knew she only wanted to have a conversation with him, but no matter how hard he tried, he couldn't think of a thing to say.

"You saw it too, didn't you, Chet?"

He blinked as he looked toward her. What did she want him to say? The expectant look in her gorgeous eyes told him he really needed to give her the courtesy of a response.

He shrugged. "Yeah, sure. I guess so."

The expectancy in her eyes changed to hurt, and he realized he'd blown it. Too frustrated to try to straighten it out, he turned back to the game and shut her out, though he couldn't help but notice when she pulled away from him and moved to her side of the bed.

CHAPTER 13

*I*t had been a long night. When the game was over, Chet had shut off the TV and then turned his back toward her. Within moments, he was snoring.

Jeneen, on the other hand, tossed and turned for hours. She prayed, she worried, she bit back tears, she got angry—and she prayed some more. Finally, sometime after 2 a.m., she'd drifted off.

The Monday-morning alarm has to be the worst sound ever, she thought as she dragged herself out of bed. A quick peek at her husband showed he was still in bed and probably still sleeping, though he no longer snored.

As she stood under the warm shower and let the water ease her into the day, she wondered if she should leave Kevin with Chet today or take him to school. They were set up on a day-to-day schedule at Sun Valley, simply because of this very dilemma. She should have thought to ask Chet last night, but their conversation hadn't exactly been very open or pleasant.

One sided, as usual. She sighed. *It hasn't always been this way. I remember when we used to lie in bed and talk for hours—about everything, about nothing. It didn't matter. We just enjoyed being together. Now . . .*

She rinsed the shampoo from her hair. *Now . . . What is going on with us now? I just wish I knew.*

She was dressed and ready to go in under thirty minutes, and as she opened the bathroom door, she hoped Chet would be awake so she could ask him what he wanted her to do about Kevin. Chet had no job to go to today, so it seemed the obvious choice to leave Kevin at home. But what if he wanted to go job hunting? He couldn't do that with a three-year-old in tow.

No TV on and no signs of life from her husband. If he didn't wake up soon, she'd have to choose the preschool by default. Of course, she could always wake him up, but she knew how grumpy that made him, and she really wasn't in the mood for anymore of his negativity or rejection at the moment.

She left the bedroom and peeked in on Kevin. He too was sleeping, clutching the corner of his blanket, but she had no qualms about waking him. Her sweet son was always ready to greet the day with a smile, even if he was still half asleep.

Tiptoeing across the room, she sat down on the edge of the bed and leaned down to kiss his soft cheek. "Good morning, sunshine" she whispered, smoothing his damp curls from his forehead. "Wake up, sleepyhead."

The boy's eyelids fluttered, but his even breathing didn't change. She kissed him again. "Want to help me make pancakes?"

Slowly his eyes opened and he turned his head to look up at her. "With syrup?"

She smiled and nodded. "Yes, with syrup. But we need to go get started."

Kevin sat up and rubbed the sleep from his eyes. "Is Daddy going to eat with us? He's not going to work anymore, right?"

Her heart twitched at his words. "Daddy will be going back to work soon, honey. Just not for a while."

"When?"

She shrugged. "We don't know, sweetheart. We'll just have to see what happens, OK? But right now we need to get going on those pancakes."

"I want Daddy to eat with us."

Jeneen nodded. "OK. Then you go on in and wake him up. How's that sound?"

Kevin's face lit up. "That sounds good!"

He jumped off the bed and headed across the hallway to wake his father

THOUGH ALL three were gathered around the table, sharing pancakes and orange juice, only Kevin seemed animated enough to try and maintain a conversation. When his topic turned to their visit to the Pritchards' home the previous day, Jeneen decided to get her son's take on Ryan's behavior.

"Did you enjoy playing with Ryan?"

He hesitated and then shrugged, his gaze fixed on his breakfast plate. "I guess. He really doesn't like to play much." Then he brightened and lifted his head. "But he sure has cool stuff in his room. He has two toy boxes!" He held up two fingers on his right hand to make his point. "Two!"

Jeneen smiled and nodded. She glanced at Chet, but he was giving his full attention to his breakfast.

She decided to try again. "But you like him, right? Ryan, I mean?"

The boy shrugged again. "I guess so. But he doesn't talk much."

From the corner of her eye, she saw Chet's head rise up for just an instant before he returned to his meal. Obviously he was wishing for a little less talk from his own family, which told her the last thing in the world he wanted was to have Kevin around today. Decision made.

"All right, Kev," she said. "Time to stop talking and finish up. You don't want to be late for school, do you?"

Kevin looked up at her, his eyes wide. "I'm going to school today?"

"It's Monday. Monday's a school day."

"But Daddy's home. I thought I was staying home with Daddy to do guy stuff."

When Chet raised his head this time, she caught just a glimpse of a smile before he swallowed it. "Not today, buddy. Sounds like your mom has other plans. And we have to do what she says, right? Besides, she doesn't think I'm very good at childcare."

He pushed back from the table and stood up. Without another word, he headed back down the hallway.

Looks like I made the wrong decision, Jeneen thought, scolding herself. *Help me to fix this, Lord.*

"You sit here and finish your breakfast, honey," she said, forcing a smile. "I'm going to go talk to Daddy for a minute. I'll be right back."

"Is Daddy mad?"

She took a deep breath. "He's not mad, honey. Daddy's fine. Now finish your breakfast, all right?"

The door to their bedroom was closed, and the TV was once again on, this time tuned to a morning news show. While the lady with the spiked blonde hair gave the weather report for the next few days—sunny and mild, light breeze, no sign of precipitation—Jeneen tried to find a way to break through her husband's self-imposed wall.

"I'm sorry, honey," she said, coming to sit next to him on the bed. "I didn't mean to imply that I didn't want Kevin to stay home with you today. I just thought you might want to go job-hunting or something, and you can't really do that with Kevin."

She waited as he continued to stare at the TV. At last he turned slowly toward her. "So that's it. You're upset because I got laid off, and you want me to hurry up and find another job. Yeah, I get it. I understand. You'd be a lot better off married to a real man, right? Someone who has a good job and goes to church and hangs out with your perfect friends." He shook his head. "Or maybe you just wish I'd stayed in the Marines and got more deployments so you'd have Kevin and the house to yourself. At least then I had a decent paycheck, and you didn't have to go out to work just to make the mortgage payment."

She swallowed a gasp as tears flooded her eyes. "Chet! How can you say that? You know how much I missed you when you were gone, and how glad I was when you finally got home. And there's no one in the world I'd rather be married to than you."

"Really?" Chet's dark eyes were cold. "Do you even know the truth yourself, Jeneen?"

Chapter 14

Ryan was sleeping in his car seat when Breanna arrived at Sun Valley Preschool and Daycare. She gently carried him inside and laid him down on one of the cots in the nap room. There were always at least one or two children sleeping there at this time of the morning. Some parents had to go to work so early that they didn't bother to wake their children, instead bringing them in asleep and placing them on a cot after a quick kiss on a soft cheek.

Breanna didn't mind. She understood how difficult it could be to wake little ones before they were ready. As a result, the school offered a light but healthy breakfast to any who needed it.

With Ryan safely tucked in for another hour or so, Breanna went to the main office to get started on some paperwork. Dani greeted her with a warm smile and a cheery hello.

"Good morning, Dani." Breanna returned the smile and slipped out of her lightweight jacket before taking a seat at her desk. "How was your weekend?"

Dani's smile widened, and Breanna marveled at the joy on her face. The young woman nearly beamed.

"I have some news," Dani announced, her brown eyes dancing.

Breanna lifted her eyebrows. "Does this news somehow involve a handsome young man named Mike?"

A slight flush crept up Dani's neck to her cheeks, and she nodded. "Yes. But don't worry—it's not an engagement announcement or anything. We both know it's way too soon for that." She brought a folding chair to Breanna's desk and took a seat beside it. "But we are excited about the possibilities in our relationship."

Breanna smiled, knowing the outgoing girl wouldn't take much encouragement to share her story. "Tell me."

Dani nodded, her blonde ponytail bobbing. "Mike and I spent a lot of time walking and talking at the beach on Saturday. It was a gorgeous day, you know."

"It certainly was. Perfect for the beach."

"Exactly. Anyway, we talked about our future plans and the things we believe God is calling us to do, and we realized how much we have in common. I'm taking classes in early childhood development, and Mike is studying to be a youth pastor. We both love children . . . ." She leaned forward and lowered her voice, no doubt to deliver the highlight of her newsflash. "And we both believe God is going to use us to work with children and youth in poverty-stricken areas of our country—or maybe even beyond."

Dani sat back in her chair and grinned. "What do you think of that?"

Breanna wasn't yet certain what she thought of Dani's news, but it was obvious Dani was excited about it. "So," she began, "you obviously believe there's a possibility that God may lead you into some sort of ministry together. Am I right so far?"

Dani nodded, more vigorously this time, and her ponytail followed suit. "Exactly! I knew you'd understand. And then Sunday, at church . . . ." She paused and drew her brows together. "I just realized I didn't see you at church yesterday. Is everything OK?"

"Yes, everything's fine. We were there, but we sat toward the back because we wanted to get out quickly and go run some errands before we went home and started dinner. We had Kevin Mason's parents over yesterday evening."

"How cool is that!"

Dani's enthusiasm seemed to extend to nearly every aspect of her life as well as other people's, and Breanna felt energized just being around her. She also appreciated the maturity level of a twenty-year-old who was willing to interrupt her own news to rejoice in someone else's.

Dani leaned forward again. "So how was your visit with Kevin's parents? He is such a super kid!"

"Yes, he is," Breanna agreed, ignoring the niggling thought that Ryan was the exact opposite of the outgoing three-year-old who had visited their home last evening. "And the visit was . . . good."

Dani raised her eyebrows. "Only good? Not great or awesome or amazing?"

Breanna chuckled. "Yes to all of the above. It was a very nice evening. We enjoyed it." *Except for Chet Mason's surliness. I'd like to think he's just quiet by nature, but I don't think that's it. He seems withdrawn at best. . . .*

Breanna switched gears. "So let's hear the rest of your news. What happened at church yesterday?"

Dani's face took on an expression that Breanna could only interpret as awe. The young woman leaned forward yet again.

"Mike and I have been visiting back and forth at one another's churches the past few weeks, but yesterday we each felt like we were supposed to go to our own churches—alone. Anyway, the services are at the same time, and when they ended and the pastor invited people to come up for prayer . . ." She took a deep breath before plunging ahead. "So we both went forward and asked for prayer. When we met for lunch later, we found out we had the same prayer requests: for God's guidance and wisdom about our future ministries and careers—and also about our relationship."

She sat back, her eyes wide, obviously waiting for Breanna's response.

"That really is amazing, isn't it?" Dani nodded. "And I know God will be faithful to answer you both. It'll be exciting to see how all this unfolds." She smiled. "I'm so pleased to know that you and Mike are handling your relationship in such a godly way. And I know God will honor that—whatever happens in your relationship or your futures."

Dani nodded again. "And the Bible tells us His plans for us are good, so as long as we stay inside those plans, our future is nothing but blessed and bright."

Blessed and bright. The words echoed in Breanna's head as she thought of Ryan. How many times lately had she wondered what sort of future the wounded little boy might have? What a great reminder that so long as they stayed within God's plan and purpose for their lives, the future was indeed blessed and bright.

By Friday Jeneen was feeling slightly encouraged and definitely relieved. Chet had mellowed a bit during the week, and he had even opened up enough to let her in once or twice. Still, their conversations tiptoed around any of the real issues Jeneen wanted to address and resolve. But quite obviously, until or unless Chet was willing to do the same, there was no sense even trying.

Kevin was so pleased that he got to stay home with his daddy today, she thought as she headed for home after a very busy day at work. *As much as he loves school, nothing tops a day devoted to "guy stuff" with his dad.*

She made a left into the housing development where they lived, relieved to be almost home. *I know Chet loves Kevin, and he's never given me any reason to doubt his ability to care of Kevin when I'm not there. But still . . .*

She let the thought fade away as she pulled into the driveway and pressed the garage door opener on her sun visor. She was pleased to see Chet's truck in its usual spot. Unless they had taken a walk to the nearby park, that meant both her men were home waiting for her.

Grabbing her purse and jacket as she climbed out of the car, she found herself thinking how good it would feel to slip off her shoes and slide into her favorite flip-flops. She smiled at the thought. It never ceased to amaze her that she lived in a part of the world where she could actually wear things like flip-flops or even shorts in early November.

Cartoons on TV and Kevin's singsong voice greeted her as she walked into the kitchen where she noticed an open jar of peanut butter and a partial loaf of bread. A knife covered in peanut butter sat next to the two items, and she shook her head. If a peanut-butter sandwich was the best Chet could do for his son's lunch, couldn't he at least put things away? She sighed and set her things down then tilted her head to try and hear what Kevin was saying. It sounded as if he were talking to someone, but if so it was a one-way conversation.

Slipping out of her shoes and not even bothering to go to her room to retrieve her flip-flops, she padded straight to the family room where she found her three-year-old on the floor, playing with his plastic animal collections. He adored the little toys that had come with his Noah's Ark set the previous Christmas and often played zoo with them.

"Hi, sweetie. I'm home," she announced, glancing around the room for some sign of Chet. Maybe he had just taken a bathroom break or something.

"Where's Daddy?" she asked as Kevin jumped up from the floor and ran to give her a hug.

"Daddy's taking a nap," Kevin announced, pulling back to give her a proud smile. "I made lunch!"

Jeneen blinked. The mess in the kitchen made more sense now, though she was less than thrilled that Chet had allowed Kevin to use a knife. She supposed it was OK so long as Chet was at his side, supervising.

She returned her son's smile. "You did? All by yourself?"

He nodded, obviously proud of his achievement. "I made one for Daddy too, but he didn't wake up to eat it."

Jeneen frowned. Didn't wake up? "You did a good job, Kev," she said. "Now you go back to your zoo animals while Mommy gets changed and . . . checks on Daddy."

When she was certain her son was once again ensconced with his toys, she made her way down the hall, hoping Chet wasn't sick. But the moment she stepped into the bedroom, her concern faded as her anger took over.

Her husband lay sprawled out on the bed, fully dressed, holding what appeared to be an empty can of beer. If it wasn't empty, it was easy to figure out where any spillage might have gone—right onto her just-back-from-the-cleaners bedspread. But from the looks of the other half-dozen or so empty cans strewn about, the can in Chet's hand was only the last of several beers he had consumed before falling into a drunken stupor.

Then she spotted the sandwich Kevin had made his daddy for lunch. It looked as if it had been cut or crunched into some sort of design, but it was unrecognizable.

Clenching her jaw she took a deep breath, wanting to unleash her anger on her irresponsible husband but knowing that wasn't the best way to handle things. How long had he been like this? The untouched, stale peanut-butter sandwich on the stand beside the bed indicated he'd been asleep at least since Kevin had decided he was hungry and had made lunch.

"That's the worst part," she grumbled as walked past the bed and into the bathroom. "What am I supposed to do about this, Lord? How do I handle it? Chet knows I don't like him drinking, especially around Kevin, but he's never done anything like this before."

She changed into a pair of jeans and a pullover top then slid her feet into the flip-flops that had been calling her name all afternoon. Leaving her husband exactly as she'd found him, she went to get Kevin and take him out for a decent meal. She'd deal with Chet later.

JENEEN AND Kevin were in the middle of a chicken dinner when Jeneen's cellphone rang. She glanced at caller ID: Chet. So he was awake at last.

As she argued with herself about answering it, Kevin asked, "Is that Daddy?"

OK, now she'd either have to lie to her son and say it wasn't, or admit that it was and answer it. She opted for the truth and accepted the call.

"So where are you?" Chet asked, his voice slurred but at least understandable.

"We're at our favorite chicken place," she said, hoping her wording included him by alluding to a place they all liked and had eaten at often. "Want to join us?"

She cringed the moment the words were out of her mouth. The last thing in the world Chet needed to do at that moment was get in his truck and drive.

"Better yet," she said before he could answer, "we're almost done. Why don't we just order you something to go and bring it home to you?"

"You're almost done? Really?" His voice now dripped with sarcasm. "How convenient. You come home and pick up our son and go out to eat without me. Aren't I good enough to go with you? Are you embarrassed to be seen with me? Is that it?"

The thought crossed Jeneen's mind that yes, she would be embarrassed to be seen with him in his current state, but she wasn't about to go there. Enough time to address the drinking and irresponsible childcare issues when she got home.

"That's not it at all, Chet," she said, keeping her voice even. "Kevin and I really are nearly through, and we can order you something and be home with it in fifteen minutes. We're not that far away."

"I know where you are. I might be useless, but I still have my memory."

Maybe that's part of the problem, Jeneen thought but again bit her tongue. "Of course you do," she said. "And I do too. I know what you like here, so I'll order and bring it home soon."

"Don't bother," he growled. "I don't need your charity. You think just because you're working and I'm not that you're better than me. But I served my country. I went through hell to keep you and Kevin safe. Do you ever think about that? About the sacrifices I made? Of course not, so don't pretend like you care, all right?"

"Chet, I—"

He cut the connection, and she sighed as she placed her phone back in her purse. Things were getting worse. If only he would agree to go to counseling, she'd happily go with him. But she knew she might as well talk to the wall as expect him to agree to something like that.

"Is Daddy coming?" Kevin's voice interrupted her thoughts.

"What, baby?" She turned to him, realizing then what he'd asked. "No, sweetheart, he's not. We'll just bring something home to him instead."

Kevin nodded and smiled, apparently satisfied with her answer. If only she and Chet could communicate so easily.

CHAPTER 15

*L*ess than thirty minutes later, Jeneen pulled into the garage and parked next to her husband's truck. She'd no sooner turned off the ignition than Kevin interrupted her silent last-minute prayer that things would go well with Chet.

"Can I take Daddy his dinner?" The bubbly three-year-old was already out of his car seat and leaning over the console to try to reach the take-out bag that rested on the front passenger seat.

Jeneen looked into his hopeful upturned face, his blue eyes dancing. "Sure." She nodded and shot up another silent prayer that Chet would at least be gracious to Kevin.

When they entered the kitchen, Jeneen reminded her son not to run in the house. She couldn't help but smile as she watched his small form, so obviously itching to run but being obedient not to, making his way down the hall toward the bedrooms.

"I got your favorite," Kevin called as he turned the knob and opened the door to his parents' room.

Jeneen was right behind him, and they both spotted Chet at the same time. It appeared he hadn't moved since they last saw him, but Jeneen noticed there were a couple more empty beer cans on the floor by the bed, so no doubt he'd gotten up long enough to retrieve them from the kitchen. The additional empty cans and the angry look on Chet's face did not bode well for his response to Kevin's announcement.

The boy stopped beside the bed and held up the bag. "Fried chicken legs—and Mom even let you have fries. They put ketchup in the bag. I saw 'em."

Jeneen hadn't realized she was holding her breath until she saw Chet offer a lopsided smile to his son. She exhaled and felt her shoulders relax.

"Thanks, buddy." Chet reached out and tousled the boys' short blond curls. "Thanks for thinking of me and getting this for me, and thanks for remembering my favorite."

Kevin turned his head and peered up at Jeneen briefly then returned his attention to Chet. "Mommy 'membered too. She's the one that got it for you." The smile in his voice faded slightly. "I didn't have any money, so I couldn't buy it."

Jeneen's heart constricted, and she was about to reassure Kevin that he'd been the one to order the meal and to carry it into the house, but Chet cut her off.

"Is that right?" Chet asked, his voice tinged with sarcasm. "Well, that makes two of us, buddy." He snorted a laugh. "I don't have any money either. What do you think of that?"

Kevin shrugged. "That's OK. Mommy has some."

The hint of sarcasm in Chet's voice heightened. "I'm sure she does." He offered a stiff smile upward toward his wife. "And you know why, buddy? Do you know why Mommy's the only one with any money around here?" He returned his gaze to Kevin and leaned closer as he spoke in a loud whisper. "It's because she's the only one who has a job." He nodded. "Yep. That's it. That's the reason Mommy has money and we don't."

He took the bag from Kevin's hand and peered inside. "Looks great," he said, directing his words toward his son. "Thanks again, buddy. You did good."

Jeneen felt her cheeks flame, but she held back the words that burned on her tongue. At least he'd had the decency to be grateful to Kevin. Still, she couldn't help but wonder how his worsening attitude of resentment toward her was affecting their son. She worried too if Kevin noticed the heavy smell of beer or the empty cans in the room.

Help us, Lord, she prayed silently. *This is not the way I want Kevin to see his father! And it certainly isn't what I expected all those months while I was praying for Chet to come home safely. Now he's here, but . . .*

She blinked back tears and cleared her throat. Time to get Kevin into the tub and ready for bed.

"HEY, WAIT a minute," Chet ordered as he watched Jeneen start to steer Kevin out of the room. "Let him stay here with me while I eat my dinner." He glared at Jeneen and hoped she got his message. "At least he doesn't mind my company."

His wife's blue eyes, so much like Kevin's, blurred with tears, and a dagger of self-condemnation zinged him in the heart. He knew she didn't deserve any of this, but sometimes he just didn't feel like stopping what he knew was destructive behavior.

"I . . . just wanted to give him his bath," Jeneen said. "It's getting late."

Chet stuffed a couple of steak fries into his mouth and watched what he knew was her discomfort as he chewed and swallowed. "It's Friday night," he said. "Let him stay up a little later. It's not like he has to go to school tomorrow."

"And Mommy doesn't have to go to work," Kevin added, looking from one parent to the other, a hopeful smile on his face.

"No, she doesn't, does she?" Chet said, taking a bite of chicken. It was barely warm, and he resisted the impulse to toss it back in the bag and make a comment about how much they must have enjoyed their hot meal—unlike him, who had to settle for nearly cold leftovers. If it hadn't been for Kevin standing between them, he would have let his mouth overrule his concern.

"That means we can do something special tomorrow, right?" Kevin again looked hopefully from one parent to the other.

Chet shrugged. "Whatever Mommy wants to do is fine with me. Remember, she's the one with the job and the money. I don't have either, so it really doesn't make any difference to me."

He waited for Jeneen to respond, to retaliate in some way, but instead she offered words of encouragement, something Chet was not in the mood for at the moment.

"You might not have a job right now, Chet," she said, a slight quiver in her voice, "but that could change any day now. You've got a lot of applications out there, and that construction job said they'd call you back as soon as work picked up."

It was obvious she didn't believe that drivel any more than he did. He tossed the now cold chicken leg back in the bag. "Well, don't hold your breath on that one," he spat. "I got a call from them just this morning, but wouldn't you know it? It wasn't about coming in to work at all. It was letting me know that they've had to lay a couple of guys off because work's so slow. They thought I'd like to know those guys would be called in ahead of me if things pick up again, so there's no sense waiting for a call that's never going to come."

Her eyes widened. From fear that he'd never work again? Could be.

He turned his head away from his family and back toward the news that had been playing in the background. He had no idea what the anchor was talking about, but he'd sure rather listen to him than to his wife and all her so-called encouragement.

"I should have died instead of Todd."

The sound of his words startled him. He hadn't meant to say them aloud. Daring to turn back to his wife and son, he saw that her face had gone straight to horrified, while Kevin's was merely confused.

He hated himself when he acted this way. What was wrong with him? Why couldn't he at least control himself for his son's sake?

He shoved his remaining fries back into the bag and waved them off. "Go away," he said. "Leave me alone for a while." Steeling his heart, he looked at Kevin. "You too, buddy. Go with Mommy and get your bath. I'll see you later."

Then he reached for the last unopened beer on the nightstand and popped it open. "Go on now. Both of you. Leave me alone—please."

He turned back to the TV and refused to acknowledge them as they left. It hurt, but not as much as knowing he was a bad influence on his son.

IT HAD taken the better part of two hours to get Kevin settled into bed and out for the night. Her heart ached for him, knowing he'd been confused and hurt by his father's actions. She'd done her best to explain them away, but the lingering look of pain in the boy's eyes told her she hadn't succeeded.

But now he was asleep, and she had no excuse not to go in and check on her husband. Still, hadn't he told them to leave him alone? There had been many times since Chet's return from deployment that she had felt unwanted in his presence, but never before had he verbalized it. And certainly never in front of Kevin.

She poured a glass of orange juice while she got up the nerve to go to her own bedroom. *How can we live like this? How long can we go on this way? If only Chet would get some help.* She sighed. He wasn't about to do that until he was convinced he had a problem and that he needed help to fix it.

When she returned the juice container to the refrigerator, she noticed the bare spot where a 12-pack of beer had sat for the last couple of days. It wasn't unusual for Chet to have one or two in the evenings, but she was certain this 12-pack had been full when she left for work this morning. Now the entire thing was gone.

Her hand trembled as she set the glass down on the counter. As much as she dreaded it, she knew she should go check on Chet, particularly now that she was aware of how much beer he'd consumed during the course of the day.

She checked the locks and turned off the lights before heading to her room. Her hand still trembled as she turned the knob and peered inside.

Chet hadn't moved, so far as she could tell, but it appeared he'd fallen asleep, propped up on pillows with the TV still flickering in front of him. She spotted a couple more empty beer cans on the bed, and for a brief moment she hoped they hadn't spilled onto the bedspread.

She pushed the thought from her mind and focused instead on trying to find out how many beers her husband had actually drunk. When she walked around to the other side of the bed, she spotted the open carton and reached inside to see how many were left.

Jeneen gasped when she realized the carton was empty.

She picked up a wastebasket and began to gather empty cans. What was Chet doing? Had that call from the construction site upset him that much? Is that why he had fallen asleep earlier and left their three-year-old son to fend for himself?

Carefully she reached for the cans lying on the bed so she could add them to the others in the wastebasket. As she stretched for the one closest to Chet, he groaned and blinked, his eyes finally opening completely and settling on Jeneen.

It didn't take long for his surprised expression to change to contempt. A chill raced up her spine as she pulled back, the final beer can in hand, and placed it in the wastebasket.

"You're awake," she said, hoping her voice sounded calmer than she felt. "Are you . . . feeling all right?"

He raised his eyebrows. "Why wouldn't I be?" He glanced at the basket full of cans in her hand and snorted. "So that's it. You think I'm drunk, don't you?"

She swallowed, praying for wisdom. "I just . . . wanted to clean up a little. It's . . . it's time for me to come to bed too."

"Really?" Sarcasm once again dripped from his words. "Well now, come on to bed then, dear wife. Come on over here and give me a kiss and tell me how much you love me."

When she didn't answer, he burst out laughing. "Yeah, right. No doubt you'd rather be anywhere than in bed with me." His eyes narrowed. "Well, don't let me stop you. If you have someplace you'd rather be, then go there. And take Kevin with you. You wouldn't want to leave him in the care of a drunk now, would you?"

Hot tears bit Jeneen's eyes. What depth of pain had been inflicted on this once gentle and loving man that he could now treat her this way? Deep down she held on to the belief that he still loved her and would one day find the healing he needed, but until then she would simply have to accept that life with Chet was not going to be easy.

She blinked the tears away and placed the nearly overflowing wastebasket in the corner. Before she could turn to make her way to the bathroom to get ready for bed, everything but the TV went dark.

Apparently Chet had turned out the light, not thinking or caring that she might like to keep that light on until she too had crawled into bed. But she decided against saying anything and pivoted to head for the bathroom. In the process, she kicked over the wastebasket, and the bevy of empty cans clattered onto the hardwood floor and rolled noisily in every direction.

Unable to hold back her tears any longer, she began to sob as she tried to pick her way toward the bathroom.

"What's wrong with you now?" Chet demanded. "What are you crying about? It's not like those cans hurt anything."

Still sobbing she managed to reach the bathroom and flipped on the light. Before she could step inside, Chet was beside her, his breath so rank that she turned her head. "I just want to go to bed, Chet. I've had a long day. . . ."

"Really?" He took her arm and turned her toward him, not hurting her but not making an effort to be gentle either. "And you think I haven't?" He was speaking just inches from her face now, and she thought she'd retch if he didn't stop. "How do you think my day was, Jeneen? You don't know? Well, I'll tell you. It was just great. Awesome, really. Especially after I found out I can't even hold on to an occasional construction job. Yeah, it was a super day."

"Please," Jeneen pleaded, turning her head away. "You've been drinking, and—"

"No kidding!" He laughed. "Well now, you're smarter than I thought, Jeneen. How'd you figure that one out, huh?" His voice rose as he leaned closer. "You're right I've been drinking, and if I had more beer, I'd keep on drinking. What do you think of that?"

Before she could answer, the bedroom door squeaked open and Kevin peeked in. "Mommy? Daddy? I'm scared."

Jeneen could hear the tears in her child's voice, and she pulled her arm free from Chet's grip and hurried to Kevin, nearly tripping over the scattered beer cans.

"It's all right, baby," she whispered, kneeling down beside him and pulling him into her arms. "Everything's OK I promise. Daddy just isn't feeling good." She stroked his hair. "Shh. It's going to be OK."

She picked him up and carried him to his room. She sat down on his bed with Kevin on her lap then rocked him as she spoke. "I'm sorry, baby. Mommy and Daddy didn't mean to scare you."

Tears pooled in her own eyes as she wondered how to handle Chet's continuing spiral into anger and depression. She was certain that's what it was, but she didn't have a clue what to do about it.

"I'm . . . sorry." Chet's voice came from the hallway. She looked up to see her husband standing just outside Kevin's room. His angry expression was gone, and he looked nearly as puzzled and wounded as Kevin had moments earlier.

"I'm truly sorry," he said again. He took a couple of tentative steps into the room. "You know I wouldn't hurt you or Mommy for anything, don't you, buddy?"

Jeneen felt Kevin's head nod before he slipped from her arms and ran to his father. Chet squatted down and pulled his son close, and her heart broke at the scene.

CHAPTER 16

After hours of tossing and turning and intermittent nightmares, Jeneen dragged herself out of bed early on Saturday morning. Chet was still asleep, and apparently so was Kevin as he hadn't come knocking on their bedroom door.

She sighed. No doubt Chet would be miserable today, suffering with a hangover that would make him even more sullen than usual. Was there any point in sticking around and trying to turn the day into a pleasant family event? She sincerely doubted it.

Once she was showered and dressed, she went to the kitchen to mix up some batter and surprise Kevin with waffles. She didn't feel like eating any herself, but she knew her son would be all smiles when he found out what was on the menu.

With the batter made, she checked her watch. Eight o'clock. That meant her mother-in-law was no doubt up and around, so it would be all right to call her.

"Mom?" she began as soon as Celia Mason answered the phone.

"Good morning, sweetheart. What a nice surprise! What are you and your boys up to this morning?"

"Oh, I, uh . . . I'm just waiting for them to wake up. I made pancake batter"

Her mother-in-law chuckled. "That grandson of mine will be a happy camper."

Jeneen smiled. "That's true." She cleared her throat. "Anyway, Mom, the reason I called is . . ." Her voice trailed off as she considered the real reason for her phone call. Though she would define it as a simple desire to drop by for a visit, it was truly so much more than that.

"I thought . . . maybe . . . that Kevin and I would . . . drop by for a visit today. Would . . . that be OK?"

"Why, of course it would. When would it not be OK to enjoy a visit from my favorite daughter-in-law and grandson?" She chuckled again then paused. "I can't imagine anything better—except having my son come along too. Has he got something else going on today?"

Jeneen thought of Chet nursing his hangover well into the afternoon and decided that technically that counted as "something else going on."

She took a deep breath. "Yeah, he does. But Kevin and I don't, and I woke up this morning thinking that it's just been too long since we spent a day together. And with Thanksgiving almost here, I thought maybe we could make some plans."

"That sounds wonderful. Yes, let's do it. Come on over as soon as Kevin has eaten his fill of pancakes. I'll make a late lunch."

"Thanks, Mom. See you soon."

She hung up the phone and sighed, wondering how much she should share with her mother-in-law. *Help me to know, Lord,* she prayed silently. *Give me wisdom, please!*

"Are we going to Grandma's today?"

Kevin's voice startled her, and she turned to find him standing in the kitchen doorway, rubbing his eyes with one hand and carrying the tattered remains of his blankie in the other. She smiled at her "grown-up" little man with his blanket.

"Yes, honey, we are. But not until after breakfast. How do pancakes sound?"

His eyes brightened. "With hot chocolate?"

Jeneen laughed. "With hot chocolate. Tell you what. You set the table while I make the pancakes, OK?"

He nodded and dropped his blankie on the floor as he scurried to the silverware drawer to get started on his assignment. Jeneen loved his enthusiasm to "help," and she had often wondered if he would still have the same enthusiasm for similar tasks when he was old enough to actually be of help.

Within moments she was scooping golden pancakes from the large skillet and dividing them up on two separate plates. As she joined Kevin at the table, she saw him staring at his father's empty seat.

"What about Daddy? You didn't make him any pancakes."

"Daddy's still sleeping, honey. He can eat later."

"But what about going to Grandma's? We should wake him up."

He started to get down from his chair, but Jeneen laid a hand on his arm. "Let's not do that, OK? Daddy needs his sleep today more than he needs pancakes."

Kevin's eyes looked doubtful, but he settled back on his chair, bowing his head and folding his hands.

She smiled. *The faith of a child . . .* "Would you like to lead our prayer, honey?"

Without looking up, he nodded, and she quickly bowed her head as he began.

"Thank You, God, for our food. And thank You for my family. But, God . . ." His voice trailed off for a moment, and Jeneen held her breath until he started again. "God, will You please help Daddy feel better? Thank You, Jesus. Amen."

Jeneen blinked away tears as she passed the syrup to her son, who lately had insisted he was too big now for her to pour it for him. *This is the same "big boy" who still clings to his security blanket.* She sighed. How it broke her heart to see him caught up in the middle of the tension between his parents.

"Mommy, you didn't make Mickey."

She stopped picking at her two partially eaten pancakes and looked at her son. "I'm sorry, sweetheart. What did you say?"

"You didn't make Mickey Mouse with the pancakes like Daddy does. He always makes Mickey with my pancakes and with peanut-butter sandwiches too." He dropped his gaze for a moment before looking back up. Sadness tinged his face. "Except yesterday when he was sleeping, and I made lunch. I don't know how to make Mickey, but I tried."

That explained the strangely shaped sandwich Kevin had left next to the bed—the sandwich Chet probably didn't even know was there.

She sighed and nodded. "I saw the sandwich you made daddy yesterday. You did a good job, honey." She patted his arm. "And you're right. I should have made your pancakes into Mickey, but I forgot. Next time, OK?"

The sadness had left his face, and he nodded. "It's OK, Mommy. They're still good."

He dove back into his breakfast, and she tried to do the same. She knew Kevin wanted his dad to wake up before they left, but Jeneen didn't. That would only complicate matters. She'd rather leave him a note and be on their way. She simply wasn't up to another confrontation this morning.

JENEEN AND Kevin pulled up in front of Celia Mason's small but welcoming home just after ten. The mid-morning sun was thin that late November day, but there were no clouds in sight and no predicted rain on the horizon.

Jeneen had scarcely undone her seatbelt before Kevin had shot out of his car seat and flung open the door. "Hold it there, Kev," she called. "I need you to help me carry something."

Kevin raced around the front of the car to stand beside her. "I'm excited to see Grandma," he announced.

She laughed. "I can tell." She walked to the now open trunk and pulled out a paper sack filled with cookie sheets. "These are Grandma's. I borrowed them to make cookies for the school bake sale because I didn't have enough, remember?"

She handed the bag to her son, who immediately turned toward the house and hurried to the front door. Jeneen slung her purse over her shoulder and followed him, once again taking advantage of his desire to "help" any way he could. She was determined to teach him to think of others and to offer assistance even when it didn't seem like a "fun" thing to do.

"We're here, Grandma!" Kevin called out as he knocked on the door as best he could while holding the bag of cookie sheets with both hands.

Chuckling, she came up behind him. "Be patient, sweetie. Grandma will get to the door as soon as she can."

She'd scarcely finished speaking when the door swung open and a woman in her late fifties, who seriously didn't look a day over forty, greeted them with a radiant smile.

"Oh, two of my very favorite people in all the world!" she exclaimed as she reached across Kevin to accept Jeneen's hug. Then she knelt down and hugged Kevin before asking, "And what have we here? It isn't Christmas yet, is it?"

Kevin laughed. "No, Grandma. It's just your cookie sheets."

Celia's dark eyes danced as she lifted her grandson off his feet, cookie sheets and all, then stood up and winked at Jeneen before saying to Kevin, "Well, that's a relief. I was wondering how I was going to make your favorite sugar cookies for Thanksgiving this year. Now that I have my cookie sheets back, my problem is solved. Let's go into the kitchen and put them away, shall we?"

Jeneen followed her mother-in-law and son into the kitchen. Celia had started her married life in this cozy two-bedroom home, and had raised her only child here after her husband died. The home held a lot of memories—and a lot of promises. Surely if a single mother, recently widowed and left with no life insurance money or marketable skills, could jump back into the workplace and somehow manage to pay the mortgage and take care of her son, then Jeneen should be able to deal with her own challenges as well . . . shouldn't she?

She shook her head and sighed. *Mom clung to You, Lord, through all those tough years. Help me to know how to do the same now.*

"I hear you had pancakes for breakfast," Celia said as she set Kevin down on his favorite chair and scooted him up to the table. "Does that mean you're too full for a chocolate doughnut?"

Jeneen laughed when she saw Kevin's face light up. "He's never too full for a chocolate doughnut, Mom, though I can't guarantee he'll eat much lunch after that."

The attractive middle-aged woman with the short salt-and-pepper hair grinned at her. "This is Grandma's house. If my grandson prefers doughnuts to lunch, then that's what he shall have." She winked at Kevin, who nodded and smiled, obviously delighted at the prospect of the treat that awaited him. Jeneen, on the other hand, reminded herself that Kevin was eating far too much junk food, and she needed to do what she could to steer him away from it—at least when Grandma wasn't involved.

In moments they were all seated around the table, Celia and Jeneen with their coffee and Kevin with his doughnut and milk.

"So," Celia said, "may I ask what was so important that my son couldn't join us today?"

"Daddy's sad," Kevin offered, speaking over a mouthful of doughnut. "I made lunch yesterday—all by myself!"

Jeneen and Celia exchanged glances, Celia's puzzled and Jeneen's flustered.

"Well, isn't that something!" Celia said. "All by yourself. You really are getting to be a big boy, aren't you? Does that mean you drove the car over here today, too?"

Kevin's eyes widened and he shook his head. "No way, Grandma. I'm just a kid."

Jeneen smiled at her son and said, "Remember, sweetheart, we don't talk with our mouth full. Swallow first."

Kevin nodded and took a gulp of milk, ending up with a white mustache on his upper lip. "I 'member, Mom."

"That was my fault," Celia said. "I should have waited till you were done." She smiled then and stood up. "Which it looks like you are. Would you like to play outside for a while?"

Kevin's eyes lit up, and he looked to Jeneen. "Can I, Mom? I'll wear my jacket."

"Sure. Just make sure you keep it zipped. It's a little nippy today." The backdoor had scarcely closed behind Kevin when Celia turned to her daughter-in-law. "What's this about Chet being sad? I know he's been moody since he got back, but is it getting worse?"

Jeneen dropped her eyes, wondering how much she could share before it crossed the line with what was appropriate to say to her husband's mother. She didn't want to be negative, but there wasn't a lot of positive going on in Chet's life right now.

She took a deep breath and lifted her head, immediately feeling herself drawn to Celia's warmth and concern. "Yeah. About that," she said. "He still hasn't found a job, as you know, but he's been filling in on temporary jobs with a local contractor. He was hoping they were going to call him back to work, but when he heard from them yesterday, it was to tell him that probably wouldn't happen." She sighed. "He . . . took it hard, Mom. Really hard."

Celia covered Jeneen's hand with her own. "I can imagine. Chet's always had a strong work ethic, and so much of his identity and self-worth is tied up in being able to provide for his family. It's only natural he'd feel bad if he can't do that."

"I know. Any man would feel bad about that. But . . ."

"But what, honey?"

The need to share this with someone pressed against her ribcage, as if her heart were demanding to be let loose. And she did trust this woman more than just about anyone else on earth.

"He's becoming . . . withdrawn," she said. "Moody. Sullen. And yesterday . . ." Her voice drifted off, and she took a deep breath before continuing. "Yesterday, while I was at work and he was supposed to be taking care of Kevin, he got drunk and passed out. That's why . . . why Kevin said he made his own lunch. By the time I got home from work yesterday afternoon, Kevin had apparently been on his own for several hours."

Unbidden tears slipped from her eyes and began to trickle down her cheeks as Celia drew her chair closer to Jeneen's and wrapped her in a hug. "On, honey, I'm so sorry. I can't imagine how hard this is on you and Kevin."

"I don't know what to do," Jeneen confessed as she literally cried on her mother-in-law's shoulder. "I've prayed. I've talked to him. I've tried to be understanding. But I honestly just don't know what to do anymore."

"We're going to get through this together," Celia promised as she stroked Jeneen's hair. "Please know that I'm here for you and Kevin—and for Chet too, of course—anytime you need me. I'm a phone call or just a few miles away. Remember that. Right now I'm going to pray for you and for the entire situation, all right?"

Jeneen nodded, relaxing as Celia's soothing words began to wash over her aching heart. At least for that moment, she began to believe there just might be a light at the end of the tunnel after all.

CHET FELT as if he were dragging himself, pull by slow and painful pull, out of a very deep and very dark hole. What was this place, and how had he ended up here?

He opened his eyes and took in the familiar scene. So he was home after all, in his own bed. Then why did he feel so awful?

I need to get to the bathroom, he thought. He wrestled with the part of himself that argued against even trying. Surely all that movement would only make him feel worse. He already felt as if his head were about to explode . . . .

Explode. The word brought a flash of light to his mind, and he shuddered. Fear clawed its way up his spine, and he nearly pulled the covers over his head and stayed where he was.

Physical need wouldn't let him. Ever so slowly, he dragged himself to a sitting position then sat for a moment on the side of the bed, breathing as deeply as he could while he waited for the room to stop spinning.

He considered calling out to Jeneen to come and help him, but he rejected that option as quickly as it had come. The last thing he wanted was for Jeneen—or worse, Kevin— to see him this way.

It took several minutes to make it to the bathroom and several more to get back to bed when he was finished. When he finally collapsed onto the bed, he was surprised at the tears that stung his eyes.

What is wrong with me? I used to be a real man, someone my wife and son respected and looked up to. Not anymore. And could he blame them? Not at all. He couldn't even get a job to support his family. The helplessness of his situation washed over him, pushing the tears from his eyes onto his cheeks. He had thought he'd seen life at its worst when he was overseas, but now he knew he'd been wrong.

CHAPTER 17

*I*t had been a pleasant Saturday, beginning with a late sleep-in and then a leisurely breakfast of omelets and fresh-squeezed orange juice. Breanna now sat in the family room with her feet up while she nursed a third cup of coffee. She knew that was probably at least one too many, but Saturday was the only day she didn't have to grab a cup on the run, either on the way to the preschool or to church.

On top of that, Steve had cleaned the kitchen and then taken Ryan to the park so she could have a break.

I am so blessed to have him, Lord. She sighed and closed her eyes. *He works all week too, even overtime when seasons change and people want their heater or air conditioner serviced. I should be giving him a mini-vacation instead of the other way around.*

She sighed. *But I know part of it is to have some alone time with Ryan. I'm pretty much with him all the time, either at home or at work, but father-son time is at a premium. If only Ryan would respond . . . even a little bit.*

Tears stung her eyes as hopelessness threatened to overwhelm her. *No!* She shook her head as if to emphasize her declaration. *I will not believe that Ryan is unreachable. He can't be!*

She swallowed the last of her coffee then got up to take the cup to the kitchen before heading outside to pull some weeds. It was the perfect fall day to work in the garden—sunny with just a hint of cool in the air. With yet another prayer for Steve and Ryan to have some sort of breakthrough moment during their time at the park, she grabbed her trowel and garden gloves from the back porch and stepped outside.

"Mommy, watch me!"

Grinning from ear to ear, Kevin climbed the steps to the top of the slide then sat down and sailed to the bottom, his blond curls blowing back from his face until he landed in the grass.

"Grandma, did you see me? Did you see how fast I went?"

Both Jeneen and Celia assured the excited three-year-old that indeed they had seen him and yes, he had truly been very fast.

Jeneen felt somewhat better after her cry and her mother-in-law's soothing words and prayer. Still, very soon she and Kevin would have to climb back in their car and go home. What would they find when they got there? The possibilities set her insides to twisting.

I love him so much, Lord. You know I do! But . . . She sighed. *I need Your wisdom and patience, Father—Your love. Because I'm running out of all that on my own.*

As if she could read her thoughts, Celia reached across the small distance between their two lawn chairs and laid a hand on Jeneen's arm. "It's going to be all right," she said.

Jeneen nodded. She knew her mother-in-law was right, but when? When would it be all right? Could she hold out until then?

"Push me, Mommy!" Kevin called out from his perch on the swing seat. "Please?"

Before she could respond, Celia squeezed her arm and called out to Kevin, "How about if your old Grandma takes a turn pushing you?" She got up from her chair and headed toward the expectant child. "I think I can still remember how to do this. Let's give it a try, shall we?"

Kevin readily agreed, and Jeneen breathed a sigh of relief. Right now she was enjoying sitting quietly in the pale sunshine, doing absolutely nothing.

CHET HAD finally managed to drag himself from the bedroom to the kitchen. Maybe getting some food into his stomach would help, though he wasn't completely convinced of that.

He had expected to find Jeneen and Kevin, but when he didn't see them in the house or the backyard, he checked in the garage. Sure enough, Jeneen's car was gone.

Frowning, he went to the coffee pot on the counter. He was relieved to see it was half-full. He'd have to heat it in the microwave, but that was easier than making a new pot.

It wasn't until he'd warmed a cup and taken it to the breakfast counter that he noticed Jeneen's note.

So, they're at my mom's. Great. No doubt she knows by now what a total loser I am—not just a jobless bum but a drunk too. He sighed. *I sure wish she was closer to her own mom and could go to her with things like that instead of dumping on mine.*

Her note had mentioned some pancake batter in the fridge, but that sounded like too much trouble. He looked in the refrigerator and found some stale pizza, no telling how old. He nuked it, choked it down with his coffee, and then headed back to bed.

CHAPTER 18

*J*eneen had dreaded returning home on Saturday evening, but she had no choice. Though she knew her mother-in-law would welcome them to stay as long as they wanted, she hadn't brought any spare clothes or personal items. Besides, she couldn't avoid Chet forever.

It was nearly dinnertime, and Jeneen thought it would be best to get home quickly now so she could have something ready for Chet in case he was feeling better and wanted to eat. She prayed nearly all the way home, but the temporary peace she'd experienced during her time with Celia had evaporated by the time she pulled her car into the garage.

"Daddy's home," Kevin announced when he saw his father's truck. "I want to play with him."

"Let's . . . let's see how he's feeling first." She didn't want to chance a confrontation that might impact her son. Better for her to run interference first.

They stepped into the kitchen and didn't hear or see any sign of Chet. Upon closer inspection she noticed some of the coffee she'd left was gone and there was a partially eaten piece of pizza on the counter. He might not be up at the moment, but apparently he had come out of the bedroom at some point.

"Kev," she said, "why don't you take your jacket into your room while I check on Daddy? You can play in there for a few minutes until I come and get you, all right?"

Kevin nodded and headed down the hallway toward his room. Jeneen took a deep breath and followed him. When she was certain he was in his room, busy playing with his Matchbox cars, she knocked softly on her own bedroom door.

No answer, but the muted sounds of the TV told her he might be awake. She opened the door and peered inside.

Chet lay on top of the covers, still wearing the clothes he'd had on the day before. A day's worth of dark stubble shadowed his jawline, and he was either asleep or wanted her to believe he was.

She sighed and walked past him to the bathroom. At least there weren't any new beer cans strewn around, but perhaps that was because he had finished them off the previous night.

When she had brushed her teeth and slipped into her pajamas, robe, and slippers, she walked out of the bathroom to find Chet sitting up in bed, leaning against his pillows but obviously wide awake.

"So you finally decided to come home," he said. "Must've run out of things to tell my mom so she'd turn against me."

Jeneen froze in place. How did she respond to such a ridiculous accusation? She knew what she wanted to say, but she thought better of it and prayed for God to keep her lips shut.

"Well?" he demanded. "Aren't you going to answer me?"

She finally managed to get her feet moving again and went to Chet's side of the bed, carefully sitting down beside him. "I was at your mom's, yes. We had a nice visit, and Kevin enjoyed himself. But no, I wasn't trying to turn your mom against you. Why would I do something like that?"

Chet shrugged. "Oh, I don't know. Just seems like you could have called your own mom and dumped on her instead of mine."

"You know I'm not close to my mom and stepdad."

Chet nodded. "Yeah, I do know that. And to tell you the truth, I think it's kind of weird—especially now. You'd think you and your parents would have reconnected when your sister died. Isn't that what a normal family would do? But you and your family didn't do that, did you?"

Jeneen knew Chet was insinuating that her family wasn't normal, and he was absolutely right. Her father had left home when his daughters were still toddlers, and they'd never heard from him again. A couple years later, her mother had married Pete, a gruff man who never had a good word to say about anyone. But as her mother used to remind her daughters regularly, "He provides for us." Jeneen supposed that was true because he went out to work at a lumberyard at least five days a week, sometimes six. He faithfully paid the bills and kept a roof over their heads, but beyond that Jeneen had never understood what her mother saw in the man.

The hardest part had been when Marilyn, Jeneen's older sister and only sibling was killed in a car accident. Marilyn was seventeen at the time, and Jeneen was devastated. She knew her mother was too, but after a few weeks Pete had insisted they stop their "blubbering" and "get over it." Jeneen never saw her mother cry again, though she imagined she grieved in private. Jeneen had done the same. What she wouldn't give to have her big sister back right now.

"Well? Aren't you going to talk to me? Don't you have anything to say?"

Several thoughts danced around in her mind, begging to be verbalized, but she ignored them all. She sighed and shook her head. "I'm sorry, Chet. I don't know what you want me to say, so I'm thinking it's better not to say anything at all. I'm going to go into the kitchen and make us all a light supper. I hope you'll join us. Our son is anxious to see you."

Chet raised his eyebrows. "Really? Well, send him in. He's always welcome around me. I love him, Jeneen."

She nodded. "I know you do. It's just—"

"Just what?" Chet interrupted. "It's just that you don't want him hanging around his loser dad? Is that it?"

Tears bit her eyes. "No. That's not it, though I will admit I don't want him hurt. If you're going to get angry and say things that will upset or confuse him, I'd rather you not spend time with him."

Chet's dark eyes narrowed. "You really think I'd do that? Seriously?"

When she didn't answer, he hollered, "Kevin? Can you hear me, buddy? Let's play for a while until your mom gets dinner ready."

Within seconds Kevin burst into the room, clutching his favorite miniature vehicles. "Can we play cars?" he asked, his eyes dancing.

"You bet we can, buddy." Chet held out his arms, and Kevin hopped up on the bed and allowed himself to be enveloped in his dad's bear hug.

Her heart twisting inside, Jeneen got up from the bed and left the room.

Sunday morning brought a return of the Santa Ana winds. Hot and dry, they raised the fire danger throughout the area and also seemed to irritate people when they hung on for several days. Breanna had seen them precipitate a higher level of agitation with the children, and she was always happy to see the winds come to an end.

But according to the weather report she'd heard while getting ready for church, that wouldn't be for several days now. She sighed as she exited the bathroom and yielded it to Steve. Meanwhile, she'd work on getting Ryan up and ready to go.

She stood in the doorway of his room, watching the fragile child's chest rise and fall. Her heart ached each time she looked at him and recognized how vulnerable and wounded he was. *Please, Father,* she prayed as she approached his bedside, *heal his heart and restore all that's been stolen from him, Lord. Show me how to love him today as You would want me to.*

Sitting down on the edge of his bed, she bent down and kissed his cheek. This was one of those times when she resisted waking him, thinking he might feel secure and loved in his dreams. But was that really the case? She imagined she'd never know until or unless Ryan decided to tell her about it.

"Time to wake up, sweetie," she whispered into his ear. "It's Sunday. Your friends in Sunday school will be waiting for you."

Instead of opening his eyes, he frowned. Breanna wondered if it was his way of denying what she'd just said. Friends? Whether in church or at Sun Valley, Ryan could be surrounded by other children and yet never make one friend. Would it always be that way?

She leaned down and slid her arms underneath him then drew him close. She loved him so much her heart ached. How could she communicate that truth to him? "Only You, Lord," she whispered. "Only You."

BREANNA WENT in to work early on Monday morning. She'd brought Ryan in asleep and laid him on a cot while she went to finish up some paperwork and got ready for the first arrivals. She'd been surprised to see Jeneen and Kevin among them. She distinctly remembered Jeneen saying last week that unless Chet found a job, he'd be keeping Kevin at home with him for a few days.

"So," she said when her gaze connected with Jeneen's, "Chet must have landed a job. That's wonderful!"

"Um, not exactly," she answered, giving Kevin a hug and kiss before he scampered off to play.

Breanna was surprised. "Then he must be hot on the trail for one, right? Can't very well take an active three-year-old on an interview, can you?"

Jeneen shook her head no and turned to leave then stopped. With tears glistening in her eyes, she turned back to Breanna and said, "I wish that's what it was. But . . ."

She paused, and Breanna sensed she was about to come undone. She laid a hand on her new friend's arm. "What is it, honey? What's wrong?"

As Breanna had anticipated, tears pushed out of Jeneen's eyes and onto her cheeks. "I just don't know what—"

The door opened, and a mother with two little ones entered, interrupting Jeneen. Rather than waiting to complete her thought, Jeneen headed for the door. With a tremble in her voice, she called over her shoulder, "See you this evening." And she was gone.

Breanna sighed and shook her head. *Oh, Lord, if it's not my business, help me to let it go. But if You want me to help, please make a way for that to happen.*

The door opened again, and another group of moms and children spilled into the office. Breanna put her concerns about Jeneen and her family in God's hands and went back to work.

CHAPTER 19

As the day drew to a close, Breanna was more than ready to pack up and go home, but she couldn't until the last child was picked up. Normally, she would ask Dani to stay and close up, but she'd given Dani the afternoon off for a special outing with Mike. Breanna believed they were taking things slowly and carefully, but she understood they needed an occasional break from their busyness just to be alone.

Quality time. She smiled. *That's what Steve always calls it when we opt for time alone.* She sighed. They could probably snag more of that quality time if Ryan were just a bit more adaptable. Leaving him anywhere, even with grandparents, sent him into a frantic crying jag that could last for days. She adored her son, and she knew Steve felt the same, but the boy was definitely high-maintenance.

Unlike Kevin over there, she thought, watching the last couple of children still waiting to be picked up as darkness snuffed out the sunlight. A stab of guilt for comparing Ryan to another child brought tears to her eyes. *Forgive me, Father . . .*

Kevin and a red-headed girl only slightly older than Kevin were hunched over a coloring book. Ryan was there, of course, but he was off in his favorite corner, stacking blocks.

Breanna blinked back the tears as the front door opened, and Breanna fully expected to see Jeneen step inside. In fact, Breanna was surprised the normally punctual mother hadn't already retrieved Kevin. But it was the little red-headed girl's mother who stopped to sign out her child and call her to her side.

"Bye, Kevin," the girl said as she scurried to her mother's outstretched arms.

Kevin looked up briefly and waved then immediately went back to his coloring project.

Breanna's heart twisted at the realization that a very friendly three-year-old and her isolated son were the only two children left, yet neither sought out the other's company.

No doubt because Kevin has given up on trying to make friends with Ryan, and Ryan has absolutely no interest whatsoever in making friends with anyone. She sighed and shook her head. *We were told about Ryan's situation with an absent father and a drug-addicted mother and the abandonment issues those experiences would no doubt raise in him. We've even read about Child Attachment Disorder, but I guess we were naïve enough to believe that once he knew we loved him unconditionally, he'd just break out of that behavior. Apparently not.*

The front door opened again, and a flustered Jeneen Mason stepped inside, her strawberry blonde hair in disarray, no doubt from the wind. Thankfully, Breanna had heard on the weather report that morning that the winds were finally dying down. That probably meant the return of cool, foggy mornings, but she preferred that to the hot dry wind.

"I am so sorry," Jeneen said as she quickly scribbled her name on the sign-out sheet. "We had some last-minute issues at work that required us all to stay until they were resolved. I should have called, but we were so busy I didn't have a chance to snag my cellphone from my purse. I'm so sorry." She glanced around the near-empty room. "Quite obviously, I've kept you here after everyone else has gone home."

Breanna smiled. "Don't worry about it. We all have unexpected things pop up at work or in our everyday lives. Can't be helped. Besides, Kevin isn't one bit of trouble."

Jeneen returned the smile as she approached Breanna. "Thank you. But I promise not to make a habit of this. I'll keep my cellphone on me during the workday so if this sort of thing ever happens again, I can call and let you know."

Breanna shook her head. "Really, Jeneen, it's not a problem." She glanced at her watch then back up at Jeneen.

"Technically, we're still open for another fifteen minutes, so I wouldn't leave before then anyway."

Breanna held the sign-out clipboard to her chest and looked over at Jeneen. "You know, Steve and I really enjoyed having you over the other day. I hope we can do it again one day soon."

"I'd like that," Jeneen agreed. "As a matter of fact, I had an idea rolling around in my head on the way over here, and I thought I'd toss it out there and see what you think."

Breanna lifted her eyebrows, intrigued. "And what might that idea be? You've got my interest."

"Well, I remember when we were at your house that you mentioned how neither you nor Steve has immediate family in the area. My parents live a few hours away, and we spent Thanksgiving with them last year. Chet was in Afghanistan, and Kevin and I brought Chet's mom with us to my parents' house. But this year my mom and stepdad are taking a cruise over Thanksgiving, and besides, we're really not that close to my family. So I've decided to cook and have my mother-in-law over. I wondered if you might like to join us—if you don't already have plans, of course."

What a lovely idea! "We don't have any plans," she admitted, "and it's getting a bit late to make any now. I was thinking it would just be Steve and Ryan and myself, but I love your idea. I'll have to talk to Steve, of course, but I'm sure he'll love it."

She paused. "But what about Chet? Is he OK with this?"

Breanna saw the flush creep up Jeneen's neck and onto her cheeks. No doubt Chet was as yet unaware of Jeneen's invitation, which was understandable since she'd said she just today started thinking about it. Both she and Steve had noticed Chet's reticence to enter into conversation, particularly if it involved answering any personal questions, so he might very well nix this entire idea.

"I . . . I'm sure he'll be . . . fine with it," Jeneen stammered. "I'll talk to him tonight and let you know."

"I'll do the same with Steve," Breanna assured her. "I hope it works out. It would be fun to spend Thanksgiving together."

"We're going to your house for Thanksgiving?" Kevin's question interrupted their conversation, and the two women looked down to see his smiling face peering up at them. "That would be so cool!"

Breanna laughed. "Actually, we'd be going to your house, Kevin. But first we have to check with your daddy and Ryan's daddy too." She tousled his hair. "We'll see what happens, all right?"

"All right!" He clapped his hands together then announced, "I'm going to go tell Ryan!"

Before either Breanna or Jeneen could say another word, he was off like a shot for the corner where Ryan sat playing with his blocks. He scarcely looked up in response to Kevin's excited chatter.

"It doesn't look like we'll have any problem convincing Kevin about this get-together," Breanna observed.

"That's for sure," Jeneen agreed. "The more the merrier, as far as he's concerned. And just this morning he mentioned that he wished you three could come to our place sometime. It's probably what gave me the idea to invite you." She smiled. "I hope it works out."

"I hope so too." She wanted to add that she couldn't imagine why it wouldn't, but something told her the event was no shoe-in with Chet Mason.

"YOU DID *what?*" Chet's dark eyes bored into hers, and she wished she could take her words back. She should have known it was a foolish idea to think her ever-increasing reclusive husband would respond well to such a request, no matter how diplomatically she'd tried to word it. She wished she'd asked him before mentioning it to Breanna, but it was too late now.

Kevin was in his room playing while she fixed a quick meal. She'd been pleasantly surprised when Chet offered to help set the table and even offered the information that he'd filled out several job applications online that day. It had seemed the perfect time to bring up Thanksgiving, but now she wondered if there really was such a thing as the perfect time when it came to Chet.

She kept her eyes on the pot as she stirred the macaroni and cheese. "I . . . I just got to thinking that since we spent last Thanksgiving at my parents' house but this year they'll be on a cruise, we might as well have your mom over here. She'll still do a lot of the baking and cooking, I'm sure, but having it here will spare her from having quite as much work And . . ." She took a deep breath. "And I'd like to invite the Pritchards too."

Chet didn't respond right away. He finished laying out the silverware and then came and stood next to her at the stove. "My mom, sure. But your new church friends? Why would you want to invite them? They're strangers."

She bit her tongue and prayed for the right words before answering. "I don't see them as strangers, Chet. She's the head of Kevin's preschool, so we see her quite often. And Steve seemed like a nice guy, don't you think? After all, you have the military background in common."

Chet snorted. "Not sure how that's a plus. But even if it were, what about their family? Don't they have somewhere else to go?"

"Not really," Jeneen answered, resisting the urge to study her husband's expression for his true feelings. "Not nearby anyway. They were just going to have Thanksgiving dinner by themselves."

"So what's wrong with that? Sounds like a good plan to me."

Jeneen squelched the frustration that threatened to take their conversation in a really bad direction and instead asked God to put a smile in her voice. "There's nothing wrong with it, honey. But since they had us over for dinner at their house, I thought it might be nice to reciprocate. I think Kevin would enjoy having Ryan over."

Chet snorted again. "I don't know why. I didn't hear the kid say one word the whole time we were there."

"Ryan is a quiet boy, that's true," Jeneen admitted. "But he'll come around. And Kevin seemed quite excited about having them over."

"You already told Kevin?"

Her cheeks grew warm, and she set down the spoon and finally looked up at her husband. "He was there when Breanna and I discussed it, so of course he overheard. I'm sorry, Chet. And if you truly don't want to do this, I'll tell her we decided it would be better another time."

Chet held her gaze for a moment before shaking his head. "I honestly don't see how it could be any better later than now. And since this will no doubt come up again until we finally do it, let's just go ahead and get it over with. Invite them for Thanksgiving, OK? Tell them I'm fine with it. I know I'm the only holdout here anyway, so let's get this on the calendar."

"Yay! Ryan's family's coming for Thanksgiving!"

The excited voice interrupted their conversation, and they turned their attention to the smiling three-year-old standing in the kitchen doorway.

"Yeah," Chet said, wearing what Jeneen knew was a forced smile. "Ryan's family is coming for Thanksgiving. What do you think of that, buddy?"

"Cool!" Kevin scampered across the kitchen floor and threw his arms around his father's legs. "Thank you, Daddy!"

Chet bent down and lifted the boy into his arms. "Don't thank me," he said, cutting his eyes toward Jeneen. "Thank your mom. This was all her idea."

Kevin transferred his attention from one parent to the other. "Thank you, Mommy. It's going to be fun!"

Jeneen smiled and nodded. "Yes, it will, sweetheart. It'll be fun." Silently, she prayed that at the very least it wouldn't turn out to be a disaster.

DANI SEEMED slightly less bubbly than usual on Wednesday morning, and Breanna sensed that something was on her mind.

"How are you doing today?" she asked when things settled down a bit during arts-and-crafts time. It was obvious the children were enjoying their activity of coloring paper turkeys.

Dani's smile was genuine but not as eager as Breanna had come to expect. "Fine," she said a bit dismissively. "Everything's good."

From the slight edge in the young woman's voice, Breanna was even more certain now that everything was definitely not "good."

"How about you?" Dani asked before turning her face back in the direction of the nearest table full of coloring children.

"Doing well, thank you." She shot up a quick prayer. "And Mike? How's he doing?"

When Dani turned toward her this time, it was if the question had melted everything else from her features and left her with a smile that was more contagious than ever.

"Mike is wonderful. Really and truly . . . wonderful."

Breanna smiled in return. Whatever was nagging at Dani apparently had nothing to do with trouble in that particular paradise. "So what are you two doing for Thanksgiving? Are you spending it together?"

Dani's smile faded. "By default, I guess we are." Her cheeks flushed. "I didn't mean that in a bad way. It's just . . ." She shrugged. "It's just a weird set of circumstances, I guess. My parents are flying back to New Jersey to visit my sister and her family. They invited me to come along, but tickets are pretty pricey right now, and traveling over Thanksgiving weekend can be a nightmare. Besides, I really did want to spend it with Mike. We'd already talked about it and planned to go to his mom's house for dinner, but then she decided at the last minute to accept her cousin's invitation to come to San Francisco for the holiday weekend. She said she hadn't seen her in a while and thought she should go. Of course, she told Mike he was welcome to come along, but he didn't want to leave me here alone."

She sighed and shrugged. "So now we're thinking we'll just go out for dinner somewhere and then go over to his place to watch some football."

Breanna very nearly opened her mouth and invited Dani and Mike to come to their place for Thanksgiving, but then she remembered they were going to Jeneen's. Hmm... Would the Masons be receptive to a couple more dinner guests? She somehow imagined Jeneen and Kevin would be fine with it, but there was no telling with Chet.

Before saying anything to anyone, she decided she'd pray about it and make up her mind later—though it couldn't be too much later because Thanksgiving was almost upon them.

An argument over Crayons erupted at the far table, and she watched Dani make a beeline in that direction. It would be delightful to finally get to spend a little time getting to know Mike, and she truly wanted to be able to see the young couple together. But was it right for her to ask Jeneen about including them? It was certainly too late to change plans and have the dinner at her house. Above all, though, she couldn't imagine Dani and Mike having Thanksgiving dinner alone at a restaurant.

She shook her head. She would think and pray about this later. Right now, she had nearly twenty rambunctious preschoolers who were no doubt getting hungry for lunch.

CHAPTER 20

*S*o when's everybody supposed to show up for this shindig?" Chet was helping Jeneen set the table, though it appeared grudgingly. He had been less than enthusiastic when she broached the subject of adding two more seats at the Thanksgiving table, but at least he hadn't said no. Kevin, of course, was thrilled to know that two of his "teachers" were coming for dinner.

"Your mom will probably get here first," she said, glancing at her watch. "It's a little after two now, so I'd say she could arrive anytime in the next hour. Breanna and Dani are each bringing a dessert, and Mom's bringing some vegetables and a salad. But she's also going to help me with all the last-minute stuff. She knows how hectic it can get right before the big meal, especially with this many guests."

Chet raised an eyebrow as he arranged the salad bowls. "You didn't have to invite so many people. I mean, it's not like somebody put a gun to your head. It could have been a nice, quiet day with just the three of us and Mom."

Jeneen's cheeks warmed. She couldn't argue with his logic, and she prayed he wouldn't become sullen or start snipping at people with his snide or sarcastic remarks. With that thought in mind, she opted not to respond as she pulled the good silverware from the door.

"Are my teachers here yet?" Kevin asked as he popped into the dining room. "I'm hungry. Can I have some pumpkin pie?"

Jeneen stopped laying silverware on each side of the plates and looked at her energetic son. "No, your teachers aren't here yet. And no, you can't have pumpkin pie because Miss Dani's bringing that. Besides, how can you possibly be hungry? You ate a huge breakfast this morning, plus you had a peanut-butter sandwich less than an hour ago."

Kevin's wide eyes went from one parent to the other and then back again. "I guess I'm just a growing boy," he announced.

Jeneen and Chet broke into laughter, and Jeneen shook her head. "Now where in the world did you hear that?"

"From Grandma." Kevin smiled, obviously pleased with himself. "And I'm still hungry."

Chet scooped his son up and then placed him on his shoulders. "Tell you what, buddy. This job here is about done, and your mom can finish up. How about if you and I go out to the backyard and play catch for a little while? If you're still hungry when we're done, maybe Mommy will let us have an apple."

Kevin grinned as he sat atop his dad's shoulders and peered at the world over the top of his head. Jeneen couldn't help but smile. This was the Chet she knew and loved, and she prayed he would stick around at least through the end of the day.

"Great idea," she said. "Get out from under my feet for a little while, and when you come back in I'll definitely have some apple slices ready for you."

Kevin's response was immediate as he declared, "Cool! Let's go, Daddy."

Jeneen and Chet exchanged glances, and she hoped he had seen the gratitude she tried to convey to him.

EXACTLY AS Jeneen had expected, Celia showed up within the hour. She placed the food she'd brought into the refrigerator and then followed Jeneen into the dining room to check the table.

"It's lovely!" she exclaimed, clapping her hands together. "I especially like the colorful paper turkey in the middle of the table."

Jeneen chuckled. "Kevin made that in preschool last week. When he brought it home, I suggested we put it on the refrigerator, but he wanted it right here. So I propped it up against the napkin holder, and it has sat there ever since."

Celia smiled and nodded. "Kevin is so like his father in some things. He's a bit more outgoing and bouncy than Chet ever was, but they're two of a kind when it comes to setting their mind to do something. I had some very interesting artwork decorating my house during his growing-up years, one of which was a turkey that looked remarkably similar to this one."

"So . . . he was somewhat introverted when he was young?"

Celia turned and fixed her dark eyes on Jeneen. "Not like he's been lately, if that's what you mean." She shook her head. "Although he wasn't as outgoing or friendly as Kevin, he certainly wasn't sullen or moody either."

Jeneen dropped her eyes before looking back up at her mother-in-law. "I see." She hesitated then continued. "Actually, I've had some serious second thoughts about having extra people here for Thanksgiving. But he and I talked about it, and he seems to be okay with it. Not crazy about it, mind you, but . . . okay."

"I'm glad." Celia took a couple of steps toward Jeneen and laid a hand on her arm. "I know my son's been through some really difficult times, and I sympathize with that. But it doesn't give him the right to lash out at others, especially his own family. You have to have a life too, and that certainly includes having friends over for a holiday dinner."

Jeneen nodded. "Thank you, Mom. I can't tell you how much your support and understanding mean to me."

Celia pulled her into a quick hug and kissed her on the cheek. "My pleasure, sweetheart. You know I consider you my daughter, and I couldn't love you more if you truly were."

She pulled back then and said, "So tell me about your other guests. What should I expect?"

Jeneen gave Celia a brief rundown on Dani and Mike—as much as she knew anyway, which wasn't much—and then on Breanna and her family.

"So you've spent time with them as a family before," Celia observed. "How did that work out?"

Jeneen shrugged. "Fine. Chet wasn't rude in any way, just relatively quiet. But to be honest, he wasn't nearly as quiet or withdrawn as Ryan. He's the same age as Kevin, but physically he's much smaller, and he scarcely ever speaks—not just to us but to his own parents. It's heartbreaking, really."

"Do you have any idea what happened to that child to make him so withdrawn?"

Jeneen shook her head. "No details. But Breanna told me his parents were both into drugs. His father was long gone before Ryan was born, and his mother died of an overdose when he was something like a year old, I believe. He's been diagnosed with Attachment Disorder."

"I'm not surprised." Celia's eyes showed a hint of tears. "Well, I do hope some of Kevin's attitude will help the poor child open up a bit."

Celia glanced toward the picture window, and Jeneen followed suit. Her two guys were playing and laughing and obviously having a good time out there. Her heart warmed at the picture.

"How long have they been out there?" Celia asked. "Long enough that they might be ready for a snack break?"

"Absolutely! In fact, I sliced up a couple of apples a little while ago. Would you like to take them out there and join your 'boys' for a while? We don't have anything we have to do in here quite yet."

Celia's smile seemed to take ten years off her already youthful appearance. "I'd love to! In fact, I was hoping you'd ask."

With that, she went to the refrigerator to retrieve the snack then headed for the backdoor, leaving Jeneen with a window of time all to herself.

She headed for the recliner in the family room, glad for even a short respite.

Mind if I join you?

The question seemed to come out of thin air, but Jeneen knew it was her Father. "Yes, please," she said aloud. "That sounds like a wonderful idea."

JENEEN CLUNG to the peace she'd felt in her short but welcome quiet time with the Lord. She'd left that place feeling encouraged and reassured, but she knew from experience how easily that could slip away in the midst of chaos or controversy.

Please don't let there be any of either, Lord, she prayed silently as everyone scooped out the potatoes, passed the veggies and the gravy, and *oohed* and *aahed* about how wonderful it all looked.

She glanced at Chet, who sat across from her, but he had lowered his head and seemed completely caught up with devouring his meal. At least he'd joined in when Steve offered thanks before the meal. Though Jeneen was relatively certain he hadn't actively participated, neither had he objected in any way. When Steve said, "amen," Kevin had shouted an "amen" of his own, and everyone had laughed, setting the perfect tone to continue through the meal.

When the conversation faded a bit as people enjoyed their meal, Celia spoke up. "So, Breanna, I know you run the daycare and preschool, but what about you, Steve? What do you do for a living?"

Steve looked up and smiled. He took a sip of water and then said, "I'm a heating and air-conditioning technician. Been doing that for a while now, basically since I got out of the Army. It was actually good old Uncle Sam who paid for my schooling to become a tech. It's a good thing too because, to be honest, I really didn't have any marketable skills when

I got out of the service. I went in soon after high school, so I was pretty young when I got out." He shrugged. "But I've never regretted it—being in the military or going to school afterward. It's worked out well."

Celia nodded. "I would imagine so. Everyone needs their heaters and air conditioners fixed at some time or other. Have you been staying busy?"

He shrugged. "Sometimes it can be a bit seasonal. Summers are really busy here in Southern California because everybody wants their AC running. But then it slows up when the seasons change and the weather cools off, but not for long. Pretty soon we're getting calls about heaters, and that stays steady until sometime in the spring."

"Interesting," Celia said. "And the Army paid for your schooling. For some reason I hadn't realized that was a possibility."

Jeneen saw Celia sneak a quick peek at her son, but Chet was still engrossed with his meal.

"And what about you, Mike?" Celia continued. "I heard Dani goes to school and works at the preschool with Breanna. What do you do?"

Mike sat to Jeneen's left, between herself and Dani. He looked up in response to Celia's question. "Right now I work at a hardware store while I'm attending the Bible college at our church. My goal is to become a youth pastor. I really like working with kids."

"And he's good at it too," Dani chimed in. "He already helps out with our church's youth group, and the kids just love him."

Mike's pale complexion took on a pinkish hue that seemed to complement his short red hair. Jeneen wondered if he might be Irish.

"Dani's the one who's really good with kids," he said. "I've seen her at Sun Valley. The kids are crazy about her."

"I'm not crazy," Kevin piped up. "But I love Miss Dani."

"See what I mean?" Mike asked as the others chuckled.

Jeneen couldn't resist peeking at Ryan. He hadn't even looked up and seemed to be playing with his food. Did he feel any affection for Dani—or anyone else for that matter? She'd never actually seen him hug or kiss Breanna or Steve, and she couldn't remember ever hearing him speak. Her heart ached for the little boy, and she could only begin to imagine how Breanna and Steve must feel.

The conversation continued in a pleasant tone as everyone chipped away at the mounds of food still sitting in the middle of table, all surrounding Kevin's paper turkey. Apparently, her son had noticed that same thing because he suddenly pointed to his artwork and asked, "Does everybody like the turkey I made?"

They all assured him they did, and he beamed. Then he turned to the only other child at the table, who sat across from him. "Ryan, you made one too. I wish you brought it."

Ryan didn't respond, though he did stop drawing lines through his mashed potatoes with his fork. It was obvious he knew the attention had turned to him. Unlike Kevin, it was also obvious he didn't like being in the spotlight.

"I imagine Ryan didn't bring his turkey because it's decorating something at his house." Jeneen caught Breanna's eye and lifted an eyebrow.

"You're absolutely right," Breanna said. "Ryan made such a beautiful turkey that we attached it to some string so we can hang it from our chandelier in the dining room. When we get our Christmas tree up, we'll take it down from the chandelier and hang it on the tree."

"Oh, cool!" Kevin declared. "Mommy, can we do that with my turkey when we get our tree?"

Jeneen smiled. "I don't see why not. But that won't be for a couple of weeks yet. Meanwhile, we'll leave it here on the table. It looks nice there, don't you think?"

Kevin agreed, and the others nodded.

The meal was nearly over, and no disasters yet. Jeneen was cautiously optimistic, though she could feel the continued tension in her shoulders and neck. She never knew when something would set Chet off; she just prayed such a thing would not pop up today.

CHAPTER 21

het thought the meal would never end. The food was good, but he wanted only two things from this day. First, to go outside and get some fresh air—and the sooner the better. And second, to wave goodbye to the last of their guests.

Even having his mother there was exhausting. He couldn't help but think she'd had that heating-and-air-conditioning-paid-by-the-Army conversation with Steve for Chet's own benefit. More than once she'd told him that he needed to get into some specific trade. Being an on-call gopher at temporary construction jobs didn't count.

Chet was relieved as they all got up and wandered away from the table, choosing to wait awhile before dessert. He knew he should either help the ladies clear the table and do the dishes, or follow Steve and Mike into the family room for some male bonding time. But as far as Chet was concerned, he'd had enough male bonding in the Marines. The last thing he wanted to do was get stuck entertaining a Bible student and an air-conditioning repairman.

Instead he began clearing the table, knowing it was just a matter of time until the women ran him off. He didn't have long to wait.

"We've got this, sweetheart," Jeneen assured him. "You go ahead and visit with the guys."

Yeah, right. Like that's going to happen. Aloud he said, "Are you sure? I don't mind helping."

All three women sent him packing, so he walked from the dining room as if he were headed to join the men but instead took a quick detour out the backdoor. The cool darkness washed over him like a liberating welcome. If only Jeneen could understand how much he did not like being smothered with other people.

The night was clear, and he sank down into a lawn chair and gazed at the blinking stars. He'd done that often during his deployment, wondering if Jeneen was watching the night sky and thinking of him. And now here he was, his wish to be reunited with his family a reality, and all he wanted was to be left alone. What was wrong with him?

He thought back over the day so far, including the near panic attack he'd had to fight off before everyone arrived. At least he'd been able to hide it from Jeneen. Then there was the excruciatingly long meal, trying to be part of the group without having to say more than absolutely necessary.

Most of all, he couldn't get away from the picture of Ryan hunched over his plate, eating little and saying nothing. Twice, though, Chet had caught the boy looking at him. The second Chet caught his gaze, the boy ducked his head. But it was the most interaction he'd seen with the little guy, including during their first visit to Steve and Breanna's.

A strange one, he thought, picturing the boy's sad brown eyes. *Glad he's not my problem.*

After a few more minutes of breathing deeply and enjoying the quiet, he forced himself back inside. He only hoped they would all eat dessert and go home soon. He wasn't sure how much longer he could hold out.

CELIA WAS the last to leave, and Jeneen breathed a huge sigh of relief as she watched her mother-in-law back out of the driveway. It had been a lovely meal and a very nice visit with all their guests, but the stress of hoping and praying Chet would stay on his best behavior until they were gone had taken its toll.

At least all the dishes were done, but now it was time to get Kevin into the tub and ready for bed. She'd ask Chet to do it, but she didn't want to add to what she imagined was already a pile of tension weighing him down.

She went to Kevin's room and found him playing with his miniature car collection. "Time for your bath," she announced. "We all had quite a day, didn't we?"

He grinned up at her. "It was fun, Mom. We should have company every day."

Jeneen chuckled. "I don't know about every day, but once in a while is nice, isn't it? Now come on, let's get those cars put away and start getting you ready for bed. It's been a long day."

It was nearly an hour later before she got her still-excited three-year-old into bed. They said their prayers, and she was about to turn out the light when he threw the covers off and started to get out of bed. "I want to say goodnight to Daddy."

She'd been expecting this request but wasn't about to let it turn into another hour of drawn-out goodnights and drinks of water and who knew what else. "You stay right there, young man," she said. "I'll go get Daddy."

She crossed the hall, expecting to find Chet watching TV in bed. But when she opened the door, she found the TV on and Chet sound asleep. Kevin would be disappointed, but she wasn't about to wake her husband up.

AT LAST Jeneen sank down onto her side of the bed, mixed emotions dancing through her mind. She was pleased at how the evening had gone, and even more pleased in how the evening had *not* gone. Chet had been fairly quiet, speaking only when spoken to, but at least he'd been cordial.

She pulled the covers up to her chin, listening to her husband's even breathing. Though she'd had misgivings about inviting extra people to dinner, it had all seemed to work out well. She liked Dani and Mike and wondered about their future. It did seem a perfect match, but who knew what God had in mind?

The other memory that had nagged at her all evening was the little conversation her mother-in-law had shared with Steve. Jeneen knew the government would spring for Chet to go to college or a trade school, but the one time she'd brought it up, he'd immediately shut her down.

Why? Why would he not want to go to school and learn a trade or get a degree so he could finally land a good job? It would be tough going for a while, but with the living allowance Chet would receive and her fulltime salary, they could make it.

She shoved it from her mind. *No sense dwelling on something that most likely will never happen. But it would be nice if it did, Lord. You could stir his heart and cause him to at least consider such a move.*

Jeneen rolled onto her side, determined to ignore the busyness in her brain and get a good night's sleep. At least she wouldn't have to cook tomorrow. Even considering the leftovers she'd sent home with all their guests, they'd still be eating turkey sandwiches and pumpkin pie for several days to come.

She'd just about drifted off when a yowl that sounded something like a wounded bear shook her back to consciousness. Jerking to a sitting position, she felt a shudder shoot up her spine as her eyes focused on Chet. He too had sat up in bed and was looking wildly about the room.

"Chet, honey," she said, laying an arm on his shoulder, "it's OK. You just—"

He shook her off and turned to stare at her. "What are you doing here?" he demanded. "How did you get in here? You'd better get away from me, you hear? I don't want to have to hurt you."

Hot tears bit her eyelids as she recoiled from her husband's words. What was wrong with him? What was he thinking? How bad a dream had it been?

"It . . . it was a dream," she said, her voice shaking. "Just a dream. Everything's OK. You're home, here with me and Kevin, where you belong." She resisted the urge to wrap her arms around him and hold him close. Quite obviously that would not be a wise move at the moment.

Chet's features began to relax slightly, and his look of fear turned to bewilderment. "Home?" he said at last. "I'm home?"

Jeneen nodded. "You're home, baby. And you're safe."

His wary gaze held hers for a moment longer. Then he held his arms out to her and began to sob.

Melting into his embrace, she comforted him in much the same way she did Kevin when he'd had an especially bad dream. She'd seen Chet cry only one time in all the years she'd known him. That was when Kevin was born. Both Jeneen and Chet had been thrilled that he was home for that monumental occasion, and it was obvious to everyone that he adored his son.

But those were tears of joy. What were these? Tears of sorrow? Of fear? Of frustration? Perhaps all those things—and more.

What is going on in your brain, Chet? At times she longed to climb inside her husband's head so she could really know what went on there, what drove him to be so different from the man she'd married. But at other times she wondered if it might destroy her to know the depth of his pain and torment.

She wanted to know; she wanted to help. Yet she somehow understood that it was bigger than anything she could fix on her own. This was worse than one of Kevin's "boo-boos" or a child's nightmare. This was a full-blown, ongoing nightmare, and she feared that it might destroy them all if they left it unaddressed much longer.

CHAPTER 22

Chet dreaded the idea of getting out of bed the next day. The day before had been bad enough, with a house full of people and no way of escape. But last night had been worse. He only vaguely remembered the nightmare that had driven him into Jeneen's arms, but he certainly remembered the humiliation he felt when he realized he was sobbing on her shoulder.

To her credit, Jeneen hadn't tried to drag him into a discussion but had limited herself to holding him and offering comforting words. But now, in the light of morning, he imagined she'd be ready to hit him with both barrels. He hoped she'd at least have the restraint not to do so in front of Kevin.

Kevin. The light of his life. But what kind of father didn't provide for his own child? It would be one thing if he knew his wife had returned to work because she wanted to, but that wasn't the case. She'd said many times how she wanted to stay home at least until Kevin was in school fulltime. But someone had to wear the pants in the family, and it obviously wasn't him.

He dragged himself from bed. The longer he waited, the more time she'd have to build her case.

The sound of cartoons drew his attention as he passed by the family room. Stopping long enough to peer through the doorway, he spotted his son, still in his pajamas and parked in front of the TV, apparently mesmerized with the antics of a cat and a mouse.

Same cartoons I used to watch, he thought. *Even my mom said she'd grown up watching them. At least there's still something that hasn't changed around here.*

He shuffled to the kitchen and spotted the half-full coffee pot on the counter. Grateful, he grabbed a mug from the cupboard and poured a cupful, though not before noticing

Jeneen sitting at the kitchen table with her prayer journal and Bible open before her.

Chet groaned inwardly. *I'm such a loser husband that my wife has to beg God for help just to get through the day. Well, for her sake I hope He's listening because He sure hasn't been around for me lately.*

He was tempted to walk right past her and take his coffee back to the bedroom, but he imagined she'd just follow him. Why not deal with this now, while Kevin was busy with his cartoons?

Plunking down in a chair across from her, he sipped his coffee and waited to see if she would start the conversation. It didn't take long.

She looked up with a smile. "Good morning, sweetheart. Did you sleep OK after . . . ?"

He knew without asking what words she had omitted from her question, so he omitted them too. "OK." He shrugged. "How about you?"

Jeneen nodded. "Fine—once I fell asleep. It took a while, though."

Here it comes. Why couldn't you fall asleep, Jeneen? I'd guess, but I don't have to because you're about to tell me, aren't you?

She reached across the table and laid her hand on his. He resisted the temptation to pull it away. No sense making this any worse than it already was.

"I love you, Chet." Her voice was low, her eyes heavy with concern. "But I'm worried about you."

He watched her take a deep breath before continuing. "You haven't been yourself since you returned from your last deployment. We both know that. I kept telling myself you just needed a little time, that things would get better soon. But they haven't. If anything, they're worse." She squeezed his hand. "What are we going to do, baby? We can't go on like this forever."

Ah, there it was—a veiled threat to fix it now or exit stage left. He knew it was coming; he just hadn't known when.

"Do you want me to leave?"

Her eyes went wide at the suddenness of his question. Slowly she pulled her hand away from his. "Why would you even ask such a thing? Of course I don't want you to leave."

He shrugged. "You said we couldn't go on like this, so what am I supposed to think?"

Slowly she shook her head. "No, Chet. No. That's not what I want at all, and that's certainly not what I meant. Did you miss the forever part? The I-love-you part?" She leaned toward him, her arms resting on her open Bible. "I meant that we need to do something to change our situation, to improve it. Chet, it's not like we don't have options or resources. That's what the VA is for, you know. You've got health benefits there for life, remember? And that doesn't mean just when you need your annual flu shot. It means now, when you're struggling with what I'm sure is PTSD, when you're having trouble finding a job, when you're withdrawing more and more from other people, especially those of us who love you. Even your mom has noticed—"

"My mom?" He leaned forward, his entire body tense. "You've been talking to my mom about this? What, you want to be sure even she knows what a loser I am? Really? You would do that?" He shook his head, his eyes fastened on hers. "I'm surprised you haven't tried to turn my own son against me."

He saw the tears pop into her blue eyes and start to glisten. He felt like the biggest jerk ever, but he couldn't bring himself to admit it or to back down. It was one thing for the two of them to have this discussion, but there was no need to bring anyone else into it.

"Oh, baby, no. I'm not trying to turn anyone against you. Your mom and I, we're just concerned because we love you, and it breaks our hearts to see you suffer this way—especially when it's not necessary. Chet, there's help available. You just have to take advantage of it. You make the appointment with the VA, and I'll even take a day off and go with you if you want." She gripped his hand again. "We can beat this together, sweetheart. And God will help us, I know it."

He yanked his hand away. "Can we at least leave God out of this? Please?" He shook his head. "And have you forgotten that I went to the VA once already, trying to get help finding a job, but it did absolutely no good. So why bother?" He shrugged. "But listen, I'll make you a deal. I'll make one more appointment with the VA—one—and then you'll leave me alone about this, OK?"

Chet watched the emotions play across his wife's face. At last she nodded. "All right. One visit, and I won't bother you again. I promise."

He felt the tension ease from his shoulders and down his spine. He'd had to compromise, but at least she'd agreed to his terms. One visit. He could handle that. And then he'd hold her to her promise if she ever dared to bring it up again.

HE SHOULD have known she wouldn't leave it alone. She'd come home from work Monday afternoon wanting to know what time his appointment with the VA would be. He'd mumbled something about not being able to get anybody on the line then promised to get it done Tuesday. She had reminded him again before she left for work the next day.

And now here it was. The appointment was made. He'd so hoped he wouldn't be able to get in for weeks or even months, and the lady on the phone who made the appointment had told him it would definitely be a bit of a wait for a regular doctor's appointment. But since he'd asked for an appointment with a counselor to discuss various issues, she'd been able to get him in that week.

Thursday, to be exact. One week since he'd had to put up with a houseful of people for the Thanksgiving meal, one week since he'd exploded from a nightmare into his wife's arms. There was a price to pay for that meltdown, and now it was here. He was just glad he'd insisted on not allowing Jeneen to accompany him.

He managed to find a parking place then headed inside. He'd grabbed his and headphones on the way out the door, something to help him pass the time while he waited to be called in. From the looks of the crowded waiting room where he now sat, it could be a while.

His favorite station was playing a new song he hadn't heard before when he noticed an old man with a scraggly beard and an even scragglier green Army jacket come shuffling into the room. As crowded as the room was, there were still about a half-dozen empty chairs to choose from, one of them right next to Chet. He sighed and shook his head as the old man picked the one next to him.

Within moments Chet was fully aware that the old man smelled even worse than he looked. Once Chet had realized where the newcomer was going to sit, he'd kept his eyes closed and listened to his music. But he couldn't ignore the offensive odor any longer. One of them was going to have to move, and since he was here first, it seemed it should be the old man's responsibility to remedy the situation.

He opened his eyes, ready to say something, but the words stuck in his throat when he made eye contact with the old man.

"Merry Christmas," the man said.

Chet lifted his eyebrows. Thanksgiving was scarcely over. He supposed the Christmas season had officially begun, but he wasn't ready for it yet.

The old man, his eyes rheumy and his skin wrinkled, still stared at him, expectant. No doubt Chet was going to have to return the greeting before he could ask the guy to leave.

He pulled the earbud from his ear and forced a smile. "And merry Christmas to you too, old-timer. Listen, I—"

The old man's eyes went wide. "Is today Christmas?" He leaned closer to Chet, ratcheting the odor level up a few notches. "I didn't miss it, did I?"

Great. He's not just old and smelly; he's senile too.

He shook his head. "No, you didn't miss Christmas. It's still a couple weeks away."

Relief seemed to wash over the old man's face; even his wrinkles relaxed a bit. He nodded. "Surely am glad to know that. Christmas is the best time of year, you know? Time for gingerbread and peace on earth. Surely wouldn't want to miss that."

"No. Surely wouldn't." Chet sighed. This wasn't going at all the way he'd expected. Maybe it would be easier just to get up and move. Asking the old man to do so seemed pointless now.

"If you'll excuse me . . ." He started to stand up, but the old man laid a hand on his arm.

"No excuse for it, boy. Anybody doesn't know what Christmas is about has no excuse for anything."

Chet groaned inwardly. Was he going to have to add "religious nut" to the terms he'd already assigned to this guy? If so, he'd move as far to the other side of the room as possible. He'd even stand against the far wall if need be.

"Don't miss it, boy. Don't miss it!" The old man was leaning so close now Chet could smell his breath. He nearly gagged but managed to keep a straight face.

"I won't," he said, trying to shake the man's hand from his arm. "I promise I won't miss it. But I've got to—"

"You've got to celebrate His birthday," the old man said, his nearly toothless grin lighting up his face. "You've got to!"

Chet nodded and pulled his arm away as he stood up. "Thanks, old-timer. Have a good day, you hear?"

He crossed to the other side of the room before the old man could answer, hoping the smelly vagrant wouldn't follow. When he plunked down in a chair between two other people, figuring that would prevent the old guy from sitting next to him again, he dared a peek in the man's direction.

CHAPTER 22   153

He was still there. Chet sighed with relief. It looked like the religious kook was about to unleash his drivel on the unlucky guy who had just taken Chet's seat.

Good luck buddy, he thought.

Chet stuck the earbud back in his ears and tried to refocus. But he couldn't keep his eyes off the old man and his new victim. They actually seemed to be having a conversation. *Wait. Are you kidding me? He's taking the old man's hands and . . . and praying with him. Seriously? Who does that?*

Apparently, the man who took Chet's seat did because the prayer continued for nearly a minute before Chet heard his name called. He turned off his music and headed toward the lady who waited in front of a set of double doors. But even as he walked, he couldn't keep his eyes off the two men praying together.

THURSDAY HAD been slower than usual at the bank, and Jeneen couldn't wait for it to end. She was out the door and on her way to pick up Kevin in under fifteen minutes. Chet had promised her he'd go to his VA appointment today, and she wanted to hear all about it.

Keep calm, she told herself. *Don't push him. Let him tell you in his own way and his own time.* But she knew it wouldn't be easy to follow her own advice.

She'd prayed about it too—many times. She was glad God was wiser and more faithful than she because if it were up to her, she'd blow it for sure.

When she arrived at the preschool, Kevin had wanted to show her something on the slide, but she'd told him it would have to wait until another time. Today they had to get home.

The minute she hit the garage door opener and saw Chet's truck in its usual place, she started praying double-time. She considered telling Kevin to go straight to his room to play while she and Daddy talked, but she decided it would be better to wait and see what happened.

When she opened the door into the kitchen, she spotted Chet standing in front of the open refrigerator, looking inside. He turned to look at them exactly as Kevin walked in the door.

"Daddy!" He ran and threw himself into his father's arms.

"Hey, buddy," Chet responded, closing the refrigerator door.

"I learned a new trick on the slide today," Kevin announced. "But Mommy couldn't watch me 'cause she was in a hurry. Will you watch me tomorrow at the park, Daddy? Please?"

Chet's gaze moved from Kevin to Jeneen. He lifted an eyebrow questioningly, no doubt asking if he could keep his son home with him the next day. She knew this was no time to deny his request.

She nodded, and Chet turned back to Kevin. "You're on, buddy. You can stay home with me tomorrow, and we'll take our lunch to the park. Then you can show me that trick, all right?"

"Yay!" Kevin threw his arms around his dad's neck, and Chet responded with a bear hug.

So, Jeneen thought, *that part was easily settled. Now if we can just find some alone time to discuss what happened at the VA today. . . .*

CHAPTER 23

*T*hat time didn't present itself until they'd finished eating and cleaning up the kitchen. After that they worked together to get Kevin settled down for the night, which was no easy task due to his excitement about spending the next day at the park with Chet.

"Are we going early, Daddy?"

Chet grinned. "Not too early, buddy. We have to let the sun come up first."

Kevin giggled. "You're silly, Daddy."

"Yes, I am. And don't you forget it." He bent down and gave the boy a final kiss, said goodnight, and left the room.

Jeneen stayed behind to pray with her son before joining Chet in their bedroom. For once he didn't have the TV on, and she sighed with relief. She waited until she was ready for bed, hoping he'd open the subject so she wouldn't have to. Crawling in beside him, she snuggled up close and asked, "So how was your day?"

"It was OK," he said, pulling her close. "And I know what you really want to know is how things went at the VA. So here's the recap. Yes, I kept my appointment, and yes, the counselor was helpful on several things. He said my records indicated I was due for a complete physical, so I set that up. Couldn't get in till after the first of the year, though. He also reminded me I can get job training— college, trade school, whatever—if I want it. They'll pay for it plus give me a monthly living allowance. It's not much, but more than I expected."

Jeneen raised up on her elbow and looked down at him. "Chet, that's great. Are you going to do it?"

He frowned. "What? Go to school?" He shrugged. "Maybe. I got a ton of paperwork to fill out and brochures to read. It'll keep me busy till way after New Year's."

She nodded. "And . . . what about the PTSD? Did he offer any suggestions about that?"

Chet sighed. "Jeneen, we don't even know if I have PTSD, OK? But yes, I did mention it. That's why he suggested the physical. That doctor can refer me to counseling . . . or whatever."

"Whatever? What does that mean?"

"You know. Support groups. Stuff like that."

"That sounds like a great idea. Can you get into one of those groups before you see your doctor?"

She could see he was getting irritated, but she couldn't seem to stop pressing. "I think getting into a support group right away would be good for you."

"Good for me, huh? Just how bad am I anyway?" He glared at her for a moment then pulled away and turned over with his back to her. "I'm tired. Good night, Jeneen."

Pain pricked her heart, and she knew she'd pushed further than she should have. But at least he'd made a doctor's appointment. It was a start. She'd have to be more careful about mentioning the support group and counseling, but she was encouraged that they'd gotten this far and had even discussed it without an actual argument.

She lay down and pulled up the covers, hoping for a good night's sleep. One more day of work this week, and then she could relax for a couple of days. She was ready for that.

THE REMAINDER of the week had been relatively uneventful. When Jeneen and Kevin got home from church on Sunday, she was looking forward to a quick lunch of leftover turkey and cranberries, followed by a quiet afternoon—maybe even a nap. When she was expecting Kevin, she took a lot of naps, but they'd been few and far between since he was born.

In short order, the three of them were sitting at the kitchen table, munching on the last of the leftover turkey while Kevin told them about what they'd learned in Sunday school that morning.

Jeneen couldn't help but take an occasional peek at Chet as Kevin talked about the giant fish swallowing Jonah. She had no doubt her husband had heard the same story when he was Kevin's age. Jeneen knew her mother-in-law had faithfully taken her only child to church every week. How was it possible that Chet no longer believed—or at least claimed he didn't? From the moment Chet and Jeneen had met, he'd never once pretended to be overly zealous about his faith, which didn't bother her at the time because she had no personal faith of her own. But by the time he returned from his first deployment, Jeneen had found that personal faith and more than once invited him to come to church with her. He'd turned her down in no uncertain terms, and his rejection had broken Celia's heart as well as Jeneen's, but both women had continued to pray that somehow God would bring Chet back.

"Daddy," Kevin said, "I wouldn't want to be in a fish's tummy, would you? It would be icky."

Chet raised his eyebrows and nodded. "I'd have to agree with you on that one, buddy. Very icky."

Jeneen was about to add her two cents worth when her cellphone rang. She seldom answered it during a meal, but she had set it on the table beside her and could see that it was Breanna calling.

"I think I'd better get this," she said, snagging the phone and punching the receive button.

"Jeneen, this is Breanna. Are you alone?"

Jeneen frowned. Why would Breanna ask such a question?

With a sense of foreboding, she excused herself from the table and went into the family room to take the call.

"I'm alone now," she said. "Breanna, what is it? What's wrong?"

"It's . . . Dani's boyfriend, Mike. Something awful has happened."

Dani swallowed, even as she sensed her heart rate rising. "What . . . what is it?"

She heard Breanna try unsuccessfully to stifle a sob. "He's . . . he's dead. A car accident...last night. Some man was drunk and . . . and he ran a red light and plowed right into Mike's car. The drunk is OK, although he's in jail, but Mike didn't have a chance."

Jeneen's knees nearly buckled as she stumbled to the couch and sank down on the cushions. "Dead?" Her voice wasn't much more than a squeak. "Mike is . . . dead? But . . . but he was just here."

"I know. That was my reaction too. Dani's mom called to tell me she wouldn't be in to work this week. I'm just glad her parents are back from their cruise. At least she's not alone."

Jeneen gripped the phone as Breanna's words began to drift together. She caught bits and pieces but didn't process most of them. The only thought that continued to roll through her mind was, how could this be? It didn't seem possible. It was just too much to wrap her mind around. She couldn't even imagine how this would affect Dani—and, in a ripple effect, how it would affect the children at Sun Valley who so loved her.

WHEN JENEEN didn't return to the table after her phone call, Chet sensed there was something wrong—particularly when he heard her go straight to their room.

"How about some cartoons?" he asked, as he used his napkin to clean his son's hands and face.

Kevin readily agreed, and Chet had him set up and tuned in within a minute. Then he headed for the bedroom. He could hear his wife's muffled sobs before he opened the door.

"What is it, baby?" He sat down on the edge of bed, just inches from where Jeneen lay on her stomach, crying into her pillow. When she didn't answer, he began to stroke her hair. "It's going to be OK, sweetheart. It's going to be OK, really. But you've got to tell me what happened."

At last she lifted her head, her eyes already beginning to swell. "It's Mike . . . Dani's boyfriend. He's . . . dead."

Chet felt his heart jumpstart. Mike? The guy who'd been at their house for Thanksgiving? The guy who wanted to be a youth pastor?

"I'm so sorry, baby," he said, holding out his arms. "What happened?"

She lifted up and moved quickly into his arms, resting her head against his chest while she tried to talk.

"Mike was . . . driving, and some guy who'd been . . . drinking . . . ran a red light . . . ."

Though Chet scarcely knew Mike, he couldn't help but think of his fellow Marines who had died during deployments to Iraq and Afghanistan. A few he'd know fairly well, some not at all. But each death chipped away a little more of his heart. Somehow this death right now seemed equally painful, though he couldn't say why.

He continued to hold his wife as he fought tears of his own, tears that had little if anything to do with Mike's death, though he could never have articulated that thought in a million years. He knew only that at that very moment, he shared his wife's pain.

CHAPTER 24

Despite a qualified substitute filling in for Dani, an almost tangible cloud hung over the preschool that Monday morning. Breanna had talked it over with her small staff, including Dani, and they all agreed that the children were simply too young to hear the news via a group announcement. Instead Breanna had typed up a brief note of explanation and planned to give a copy to all the parents when they came to pick up their children. In the note, she had not only explained what happened but also encouraged parents to share with her any questions or concerns they might have. Finally, she had left it to the individual parents to deal with the issue in whatever way seemed most appropriate to them.

Still, she couldn't help but think the children would sense something was wrong, particularly when Dani didn't come in for a few days. Breanna had told her to take as long as she needed, but she knew several of the kids were especially attached to Dani. If the preschool had been established as a Christian facility, she could incorporate something about Mike being in heaven with Jesus, but the school was secular with students of various religious faiths—or none at all. No doubt this was going to be a difficult transition for all of them.

Her eyes moved to Ryan's favorite corner, where she saw him playing with the same toys he had played with last week and the week before and—

She shook her head. *We have enough to deal with right now; no sense adding my concerns about Ryan into the mix.*

A tug on her pant leg interrupted her thoughts. She looked down to find a little girl with huge dark eyes looking up at her.

"What is it, Anabelle?" she asked, bending down to speak to her face to face.

"My tummy hurts."

Breanna felt the girl's forehead. No fever. "All right, sweetie," she said, standing up and taking Anabelle by the hand. "Let's go put you down on a cot for a little while and see how you feel then, all right? If you don't get better, we'll call your mommy to come and get you."

Anabelle nodded and willingly accompanied Breanna to the back room. Once on the cot, she gripped the edge of the blanket and held it close enough that she could suck her thumb.

Breanna's heart twisted at the child's vulnerability, though she'd handled situations like this more times than she could count. Most often the child felt better after a short nap, but occasionally she had to call a parent to come and retrieve an ailing child. It all went with the territory.

The situation with Dani was a lot tougher. Though the children, with the exception of Ryan and Kevin, had never met Mike, most of the students at Sun Valley adored Dani. When Dani returned to work, would she be able to remain upbeat and cheerful throughout the day? Breanna's heart ached at the thought of how tough all of this would be on the young woman she had come to love and admire.

She glanced back at Ryan. Sometimes life just didn't seem fair. Then again, God never promised it would be. She sighed. *Whether life is fair or not, I know You are good, Lord . . . all the time.*

BY THE time Jeneen made it home from work on Monday, her nerves and muscles felt stretched to the breaking point. If Mike's death had affected her this deeply, she couldn't imagine how shattered Dani must feel. *Thank goodness Kevin stayed home with Chet today. I imagine the mood at Sun Valley is a bit uncomfortable right now, even if the kids don't know what happened. I sure don't envy Breanna having to handle this.*

She forced a smile as she stepped into the kitchen and called out a greeting. "Hey, you two, I'm home!"

Kevin's return greeting came from the direction of his room, followed almost immediately by pounding footsteps down the hallway. She bent down when the three-year-old burst into the kitchen and launched himself into her arms.

"Hey, slow down, buddy," she said, holding him close. "Remember, no running in the house."

He pulled back and looked into her eyes, his face nearly glowing. "Daddy and I had such a fun day! You wouldn't believe it, Mom. We made peanut-butter sandwiches and took 'em to the park, and we played on the slide and the swings and in the sand, and then we came home and played cars in my room."

"Wow, that really does sound like a fun day," she said, pulling him close for a quick kiss on his cheek.

Kevin nodded. "It was. Come on, Mom. Come and see the racetrack we made in the bedroom."

Laughing in spite of her earlier somber mood, Jeneen obediently followed her excited son.

"Look, Daddy," he announced when they arrived in the doorway. "Mommy's home!"

Chet looked up from the floor where he was surrounded by Matchbox vehicles and a makeshift cardboard racetrack. "So I see," he said, his smile appearing genuine. "You going to join us on the floor, Mommy?"

Jeneen laughed again and shook her head. "Some other time. I put a meatloaf together before I left for work this morning, and I'm going to go put it in the oven now and then peel some potatoes. I'll be back later."

Chet shrugged. "Suit yourself. You don't know what you're missing."

His dark eyes twinkled, and Jeneen felt her heart soar as it always did when she caught occasional glimpses of the man she'd fallen in love with and married.

Kevin looked from her to Chet then and said, "Maybe we should let her go fix dinner, Daddy. I'm starved!"

Both Chet and Jeneen laughed, as Chet shook his head and went back to playing with the toys on the floor and Jeneen turned around and left the room.

THEY'D SCARCELY finished eating when the doorbell rang.

"I wonder who that could be." Jeneen frowned and started to get up, but Chet waved her back into her chair.

"I'll get it," he said, feeling the need to protect his family rise up inside him. He knew it was ridiculous to compare the arrival of unexpected guests to many of the dangers he'd faced in Afghanistan, but he couldn't seem to get past that sense of alarm that triggered in him over just about anything that resembled a surprise. Until he could check it out and convince himself that all was well, he remained on edge.

He relaxed when he opened the front door to find Breanna, Ryan in her arms, standing on the front porch. He was about to offer a greeting and a welcome when the normally bouncy redhead spoke up first.

"I'm sorry to come unannounced," she said. "I left my cellphone at work, or I would have called first."

"No problem," Chet said, shrugging his shoulders. "Come on in. Jeneen and Kevin are in the kitchen."

She shook her head. "I was afraid of that. I don't want to interrupt your dinner."

"Hey, we're done. No interruption at all." He opened the door all the way and stepped back so they could come inside.

As Jeneen passed by, Chet's eyes caught Ryan's, and he offered a smile, wondering if the boy would return the gesture. He didn't. Slamming his eyes shut, the boy shoved his thumb into his mouth and seemed to burrow deeper into his mother's shoulder.

Chet closed the door and led their guests into the kitchen. "Look who's here," he announced, picking up his empty plate and carrying it to the sink. "Go ahead and take my place," he said to Breanna. "Kevin and I were about to go back to playing cars in his room." He shifted his glance to Ryan, still nestled in his mother's arms. "Want to come, Ryan?"

The boy didn't respond, but when Breanna set the child down and physically placed Ryan's hand in Chet's, he willingly followed.

CHAPTER 25

Jeneen watched Chet lead the boys from the kitchen toward the hallway, and again she realized how wonderful her husband could be when he wasn't in the grips of his PTSD—or whatever he wanted to believe it was.

"He's good with them, isn't he?" Breanna observed.

Jeneen turned to her friend and nodded. "He is." She indicated the still partially set table. "Have you two eaten? There's plenty here if you haven't."

Breanna held up her hand and shook her head. "Oh, no, really. We grabbed something just before we came. Steve's got a meeting at church tonight, so I figured it was easier if Ryan and I stopped on the way. Thanks for the offer, though."

"How about a cup of tea? The water's already hot. I was about to fix some for myself."

"That would be nice. Thanks."

With their steaming mugs in front of them, the women sat at the table and faced one another.

"What's up?" Jeneen asked. When Breanna lifted her gaze, there were tears in her eyes.

"It was such a hard day today." She shook her head. "I wanted so much to be able to bring all the children together and talk to them about Dani's friend Mike being in heaven with Jesus, but I can't do that. It makes me wonder if I made a terrible mistake by establishing a secular school instead of a private Christian one."

Jeneen reached across the table and covered Breanna's hand with her own. "I haven't known you long, but I know you well enough to be sure that you prayed long and hard before launching Sun Valley. Therefore I have to believe that God directed you to establish it exactly as you did." She leaned forward. "Though it would be nice to be able to pray with the children and tell them Bible stories, maybe God wants you to reach out to those who don't yet know Him. You're such a warm and positive witness for God's love, Breanna. I sensed that in you the moment I met you."

Breanna offered a weak smile. "Maybe that's because you're a Christian too. Several of the parents who bring their children to Sun Valley are believers, but the majority aren't. They're the ones I want so desperately to reach, but today I wondered if I'd had any impact at all—on any of them."

Jeneen squeezed her hand. "Of course you have. God wouldn't have planted you there if He didn't plan to use you."

Tears pooled in Breanna's green eyes. "Somehow I knew you'd know just what to say." She sighed. "Thank you for being such a good friend—to all of us, even Ryan. I know it doesn't look like it, but I actually believe he was OK with coming here. He would have continued clinging to me like Velcro if he weren't."

Jeneen chuckled. "He's a sweetheart—Velcro or not. And you and your family are welcome to drop by here anytime."

"The same goes for you," Breanna added. "We need to have you all over to our place again soon."

Jeneen nodded, as she felt a sudden tugging in her heart. "Would you like me to pray for you?" she offered.

"Would you?" Breanna asked. "I'd love that, yes. With Steve gone this evening, I need someone to pray with me."

They clasped their hands together on top of the table, closed their eyes, and bowed their heads, as Jeneen began to speak to their Father.

THE MEMORIAL service was held on Saturday, a week to the day since Mike died. The church he'd attended was packed with congregants, family members, coworkers, and friends. Jeneen had been pleasantly surprised when Chet agreed to come along. They sat next to the Pritchards, and Jeneen couldn't help but compare the quiet, perfectly still Ryan to her own fidgety son. Quiet was easier to manage, but she knew Breanna would love for her son to fidget and chatter on occasion. The pain locked inside the little boy was beyond her comprehension.

As the pastor shared about Mike's life and his devotion to serving Christ, Jeneen glanced from the corner of her eye at her husband, who sat nearest the aisle, just on the other side of their son. Chet seemed nearly as still and quiet as Ryan. Not a word, not a gesture, not a movement. Was he listening? As the pastor talked more about Mike's devotion to his Lord, she couldn't help but think of the many times Chet had surely heard similar messages during his growing-up years. Celia had told Jeneen that when Chet was little, he'd loved going to Sunday school and hearing Bible stories. Even later, when he and Jeneen were first married, he still claimed to believe in God, though his faith seemed more an afterthought than a reality. And of course, since Jeneen hadn't been a true believer then, Chet's lack of passion for his faith hadn't seemed odd to her at all.

Now, since his second return from the Middle East, all that had changed. She hadn't once heard her husband mention God unless it was to scoff at His so-called "faithfulness."

Touch Chet's heart, Lord, she prayed silently. *Draw him back to You, please, Father!*

Jeneen turned her attention to Kevin. The little boy's face seemed to glow as he listened to the pastor talk about heaven. Though he wiggled occasionally, he appeared to be taking it all in.

The faith of a child, she thought, even as Ryan's face came to mind. What did that sad little boy, sitting statue-still between his adoptive parents, think or believe? How terribly had he been damaged before coming to live with Breanna and Steve?

Father, reach that sweet child, please. Bring healing to his precious heart.

A sense of peace washed over her then, bringing unexpected tears to her eyes. But she recognized they weren't tears of sadness or grief over Mike's passing, but rather tears of joy that God was present with them, today and always, no matter how difficult the situation might be.

CHET DROVE his family home in silence. He'd managed to hold himself together through the memorial service and the gathering in the church fellowship hall afterward. He was relatively certain he'd said all the necessary right things and avoided saying anything wrong, but he'd been unable to eat any of the countless dishes stacked on several serving tables.

Having spent most of his time standing around trying to appear polite and caring, he'd overheard that Mike's parents would be having another memorial service at their own church in another state, the one Mike had attended growing up. When he'd briefly spoken to Dani, she'd tearfully told him she'd be flying out to stay with Mike's parents for a few days so she could attend the service there as well.

Chet frowned as he turned into their driveway and hit the garage door opener. Though he'd noticed Dani carrying a hankie throughout the day and using it often to mop her tears, he'd also noticed she'd had an almost tangible peace about her. That puzzled him. Had he been wrong in thinking that Dani and Mike seemed close when he saw them together at Thanksgiving? He didn't think so. And yet Dani seemed to be dealing with Mike's death better than he would have expected.

Kevin had fallen asleep on the way home, and while Jeneen unlocked the door and stepped into the kitchen, Chet lifted Kevin from his car seat and carried him inside.

"I'll put him down for a nap," he said softly as he passed by Jeneen. She nodded and squeezed his arm. Though she hadn't said a word, he somehow knew she shared his fresh reminder of how short and precious life could be. He hugged Kevin just a little tighter, even as his mind pulled up an image of Ryan and his big sad eyes.

CHAPTER 26

By the time the Sunday morning church service had ended, Jeneen had begun to wonder if she was coming down with something. She felt a bit weak and lightheaded, and her throat was scratchy. But she was certain she didn't have a fever, so she didn't mention it. Instead, she and Kevin picked up a bucket of broiled chicken and some cole slaw on their way home, a meal all three of them enjoyed.

Chet was up and dressed and waiting for them when they returned home. In minutes, they were seated around the kitchen table, eating their lunch.

"You look cheerful today," Jeneen commented as she studied her husband's face.

He lifted his eyebrows. "Does that mean I'm usually not?"

Jeneen hoped he was teasing with that question and not becoming defensive. "Not at all." She shrugged. "It's just that today you seem . . . more so than usual."

Chet grinned, and Jeneen felt the tension release in her neck and shoulders.

"Maybe that's because I got a call from one of my buddies at a different construction company than I was working for a couple weeks ago." His grin widened, and his dark eyes danced. "He says they might be hiring soon, and he wondered if I wanted to come by and apply tomorrow."

"Oh, Chet, that's wonderful!" Jeneen reached across the table and took his hand. "I knew something would turn up."

Chet's smile faded. "I haven't got the job yet, you know. It's only a maybe right now. But thanks to my buddy giving me a heads-up, I'll be able to get over there and apply before they start actively looking."

Jeneen's heart soared. This was exactly what her husband needed—well, at least one of the things he needed. She knew he also needed to get into some sort of counseling and support group for what she was sure was PTSD; most of all he needed to return to the faith of his youth, to the Lord he once claimed to know and love. But for now she'd rejoice in this one breakthrough and pray it ended with permanent employment for Chet.

Kevin sneezed, interrupting her thoughts. She felt his forehead—slightly warm. She'd better keep an eye on him, especially now during cold and flu season.

JENEEN WOKE up in the early-morning hours, long before the alarm was set to go off. Her throat ached, her head pounded, and her nose dripped. She was relatively certain she didn't have the flu, as they'd all gotten their flu shots. But a doozy of a cold? She sighed. Yes, that's definitely what it felt like. It might even explain Kevin's sneezing yesterday.

She got up and went into the bathroom to get a couple of over-the-counter cold pills. Then she took her temperature and confirmed she had a slight fever. By the time she returned to bed, Chet was awake.

"What's up?" he asked, propped up on his elbows. "You OK?"

She climbed back into bed. "I'm afraid I've got a cold. I don't feel horrible but bad enough that it might be best if I stay home for a day or two. I sure don't want to pass it around to anyone else. We'll keep Kevin home from school, too, since I heard him sneezing yesterday, so he might be coming down with something too." She sighed. "You might have to take over most of the childcare around here for the next few days."

"That's not a problem," he said, "except I need to break away long enough to go apply for that job in the morning. Tell you what. Why don't you sleep in? If Kevin's feeling OK, I'll get him ready for school and drop him off on my way to the construction site. Then when I'm through there, I'll swing by and pick him up. That way you can get some rest. Of course, if he's sick too, I'll have to leave him here with you."

She nodded and resisted the impulse to snuggle up close to him. "I'd hug you, but I don't want to risk sharing this cold with you—especially when there's a good chance you might be going back to work soon." She smiled as she lay back against the pillows. "And I have to admit, your plan to leave Kevin at school while you're applying for that job is an excellent one—unless he's sick, of course. Thank you, sweetheart."

Chet lay down then, and within moments he was snoring.

She smiled and rolled over, hoping she could fall asleep half as easily.

CHET FELT as if someone had poked the biggest pin imaginable into his bubble. Then again, it had been his own fault for getting his hopes up and counting on something that was only a possibility.

When he and Jeneen decided Kevin wasn't sick after all, Chet had dropped the boy at school and made it to the construction site before eight, thinking he was early enough to be one of the first applicants. Yet when he stepped into the small trailer that served as an office, he found standing-room only. Seemed he wasn't the only one out of work and desperate to snag a paycheck.

Along with a dozen other hopefuls, he'd filled out and turned in an application, though he knew it was pointless. At the top of the application form was a statement declaring that union members in good standing would get the first consideration. As usual, that left him out.

RETURN TO CHRISTMAS

Despondent, he headed home. How was he going to tell Jeneen he'd failed again? How long would she hold on to their marriage before she got tired of being the only bread-winner in the family?

Tears stung his eyes then, but he brushed them away as arrived back home. The last thing Jeneen needed was a worthless, cry-baby husband with absolutely nothing to offer her.

The house was quiet when he stepped inside. Good. That probably meant she was still asleep.

As he walked down the hall toward their room, he caught a glimpse of Kevin's room, complete with unmade bed, something Jeneen would never allow if she'd been the one getting their son ready for the day.

He stopped, his hand on his bedroom doorknob. Kevin! He'd been so self-absorbed with his disappoint-ment over the situation at the construction site that he'd completely forgotten about his son.

Opening the door and peeking inside to confirm Jeneen was still asleep, he then reclosed the door as quietly as possible and hurried back toward the garage, silently calling himself every negative name he could imagine.

CHAPTER 27

By Wednesday, Jeneen was feeling well enough to return to work, and thankfully it seemed neither Chet nor Kevin had caught her cold. She had noticed, however, that her husband's pleasant mood of recent days had now been replaced with one of sullenness. For the life of her, she couldn't imagine what might have happened to precipitate such a drastic change—unless things hadn't gone as well as he'd indicated at the construction company.

Both of her "boys" had stayed home today, though she'd offered to take Kevin to school in case Chet got a call to come in for an interview. He'd rejected her offer, though, saying that if he did get a call he could always take Kevin to school then. The way he'd said it, though, sounded to Jeneen as if he had little or no expectation of receiving such a call.

She pulled into the bank parking lot and left the motor running so she could feel the heat. Though the weather had remained pleasant and mild the past few days, nights and early mornings were nippy.

Still gripping the top of her steering wheel, she laid her head on top of her hands. *What is it, Father? What's going on with Chet? Did something happen that I should know about, or is it just more of the same moodiness that's been plaguing him for months now? What should I do? What can I do? Show me, Lord. Please!*

She jumped at the sound of a honking horn and looked up to see one of the other bank employees pulling up beside her. She forced herself to smile and wave at the older woman, and then she shut off the motor and prepared to exit her car and take on the day.

"Daddy, can we get our Christmas tree today? Please?"

Chet jerked from a deep sleep and blinked at the morning light. He forced his eyes open and focused them on his son, who stood beside the bed smiling and still in his pajamas. Immediate guilt washed over him. He should have been the one to awaken his son, not the other way around. No wonder Jeneen preferred to leave Kevin with professionals.

"Can we, Daddy? Please?"

It was obvious his son's request wasn't going away any time soon, and even as Chet considered his options, going to get a Christmas tree that day sounded like a good one.

He yawned and sat up. "Sure," he said, tousling the three-year-old's blond locks. "I don't see why not."

Kevin shrieked with joy and started bouncing up and down. "Can I pick it out, Daddy? Can I?"

Chet stretched and yawned again. "How about if we pick it out together? We'll keep looking until we find one we both like. Sound like a good plan?"

It was obvious Kevin thought it was a great plan as he threw himself into his father's arms. Chet pulled him up onto his lap.

"Can we get a big one?" the boy asked, his upturned face glowing and his blue eyes dancing.

Chet laughed, his negative feelings of guilt washing away in the wake of his son's bubbly personality. "We'll see, buddy. Remember, it has to fit in the house, and we need enough room on top to put your favorite star decoration. And besides, we can't go until we're dressed and have a good breakfast. What would you like this morning?"

"Pancakes!"

Not surprised, Chet nodded. "OK, pancakes it is. But first you go get dressed in the clothes Mommy laid out for you last night. I'll take a quick shower, and then we'll get those pancakes going."

"Yay! Oh, Daddy, I'm so glad you're here with me instead of working." Kevin jumped down off Chet's lap and charged out of the room and into his. Chet didn't even bother to remind him not to run in the house.

With a sigh, Chet pulled himself up on his feet and headed for the shower. Kevin might be happy that his daddy wasn't working, but Chet sure wasn't. He imagined Jeneen wasn't either.

I haven't even told her I forgot Kevin at school the other day. He shook his head and reached in to turn on the shower. *What kind of man can't find a job and then forgets to pick up his own kid?*

He stepped into the shower and let the warm water wash over him, wishing it could wash away his feelings of failure.

JENEEN CAME home that afternoon to find a beautiful Douglas Fir standing in front of the picture window in the family room. Boxes of decorations sat on the floor beside it, and Kevin was parked in front of the TV watching cartoons. Chet was snoozing on the couch.

"Hi, sweetie," she said, bending down to kiss the top of Kevin's head. "Looks like you and Daddy have been busy today."

Kevin jumped up and pointed at the tree. "Did you see our Christmas tree? Daddy and I picked it out together, but he didn't want to decorate it. He said you do a better job. Can I help?"

Jeneen glanced toward Chet as he sat up and rubbed his eyes. He wasn't smiling, but she hoped that was because he wasn't quite awake yet.

She turned her attention back to Kevin. "Of course you can help. I don't see how I could do it without you."

Kevin threw his arms around her legs. "Thank you, Mommy! Can we do it now?"

She chuckled and looked again at her husband. He still wasn't smiling.

"How about if we eat first?" she suggested as she lifted her son into her arms. "I'm hungry, aren't you?"

Kevin shook his head. "If we decorate the tree first, then I'll be hungry."

Jeneen kissed his forehead and smoothed a couple of curls away from his face. "Sorry, Kev, but we're going to eat first. I'll keep it simple. Vegetable soup and grilled cheese sandwiches. What do you think?"

The boy's smile was tentative. "Could we have peanut butter instead?"

Jeneen sighed and looked toward Chet. "Something tells me that's what you had for lunch."

Expressionless, Chet nodded, confirming her suspicions.

"All right then," she said, putting Kevin down, "soup and grilled cheese it is. Come on. Let's go into the kitchen, and you can help me."

As mother and son headed out of the room, Jeneen glanced back at her husband. He hadn't moved but sat on the edge of the couch, his head in his hands. It was obvious something was going on, but she doubted she was going to be able to get it out of him.

She handed Kevin some paper plates and told him to set the table while she grabbed some cheese and bread from the fridge. In minutes the soup and sandwiches were ready, and the table was set.

"Guess we'd better go get Daddy," she said, smiling at Kevin.

The excited expression the boy had worn since she'd gotten home now faded. He got what she often thought of as his "grown-up look" and sighed.

"I think Daddy's sad," he said. "We had lots of fun today, but Daddy didn't laugh. I tried to be good, but it didn't help."

"Oh, honey!" She scooped her son into her arms. "It's not your fault when Mommy or Daddy is sad, OK?" She smiled and pulled him close. "Now let's go get Daddy and see if some food will cheer him up."

Kevin nodded as she set him back down, but he looked dubious.

When they walked into the family room, the couch was empty, and Jeneen's heart sank. "He must be in the bedroom," she said, forcing a cheery note into her voice. "Why don't you go wash your hands while I get Daddy?"

Kevin headed down the hall to the bathroom while Jeneen went to her own room, praying all the way. She was surprised when she opened the door to find Chet asleep on top of the covers, with both the light and the TV off.

She closed the door quietly behind her and went back to the kitchen. She needed to get Kevin fed then help him decorate the tree before his bedtime. When all that was finished, she'd see what she could do about having a heart-to-heart talk with her husband—even if she had to wake him from a sound sleep to do it.

Chapter 28

She was certain Chet was ignoring her by pretending to be asleep, but she was determined to force the issue. His mood swings were nearly out of control, and she didn't know how much longer the three of them could continue this way.

"Chet." She touched his shoulder. "Chet, please, open your eyes. I need to talk to you."

When he didn't respond, she turned away in frustration and nearly tripped over his jeans lying in the middle of the floor. Irritated, she huffed when she picked them up and laid them across the chair in the corner. Then she spotted a little white business card that had apparently fallen from his pocket.

She picked it up, ready to put it on the dresser when she glanced at the wording: "PTSD support group" and a man's name and number.

Jeneen returned to her husband's bedside, more determined than ever to get him to talk to her.

"Chet," she said, her voice louder now.

She reached down and shook his shoulder. "I know you're not sleeping. Open your eyes and talk to me because I'm not going away until you do."

She watched his chest heave in a sigh before his dark eyes finally opened. "All right," he said. "Fine. Let's get it over with. What do you want to talk about?"

Forcing herself to remain calm, she sat down on the edge of the bed. "Us." She waited, watching his eyes for a change. When none came, she continued. "We're a family, Chet—you, me, and Kevin. And sometimes it still feels that way—when you're in a good mood for whatever reason. But when you're like this . . ." Her voice drifted off, and she shook her head. "When you're like this,

I feel like you're farther away from me than when you were in Afghanistan."

Tears bit her eyes. "We can't go on this way, Chet. We've got to get some help, some counseling, or—"

"I told you," he said, interrupting, "I have an appointment to see the doctor after the first of the year. I can't get in until then."

Jeneen held up the card. "But you could call this number and get some help now."

He frowned. "What's that?"

"It fell out of your pocket. It's a name and number to call for a PTSD support group. I assume you got it when you went to the VA."

"So you've been going through my pockets."

She shook her head. "I told you. It must have fallen out because I found it on the floor where you left your pants."

"Whatever." He rolled over and turned his back to her. "I'm not going to some group of misfits and cry-babies and listen to them whine about their feelings. And I'm sure not going to join them. Now leave me alone."

Her heart twisted as the tears spilled over onto her cheeks. Then she stood up and headed for the bathroom. She might as well get ready for bed. She had to go to work in the morning. And with Chet behaving as he was, she decided it would be better if she took Kevin to preschool so he could play with his friends.

BREANNA SPOTTED Jeneen and Kevin as soon as they walked in. On first inspection, it seemed a lingering sleepiness hovered over the heavy-eyed child, but the moment he spotted James and Mark, his face lit up. After a quick good-bye hug and kiss with his mom, he was off to join his two best buddies.

"Good morning," Breanna said as she approached Jeneen, who was signing the attendance sheet for her son. "How are you doing? We've missed you the last few days."

Jeneen looked up and nodded, though her smile looked weary. "I've been leaving Kevin home with Chet, but I decided it would be better for him to . . . to come here today."

She dropped her eyes for a moment before looking back up, and Breanna thought she saw tears in them before she blinked them away.

"Everything OK?" Breanna asked.

Jeneen sighed, and her smile disappeared. As if checking to make sure no one else was in earshot, she glanced around before adding, "It's . . . Chet. Just when I think we're making progress and his moods are somewhat improved, he turns on a dime and ends up angrier or more sullen than before. I never know what's going to set him off, or how deep he'll go when he withdraws." She shrugged and shook her head. "Honestly, Breanna, I don't know what to do anymore. He's been to the VA, but they can't get him in for an appointment for a few weeks yet. And he won't even consider going to a support group."

The tears Breanna had thought she'd seen earlier were back, and she reached out and laid her hand on Jeneen's arm. "I'm so sorry. I can't even begin to imagine how difficult this is for you." An image of her own son flashed through her mind. "I do know a little about withdrawal, though. That seems to be an almost constant condition for Ryan." She shook her head. "Still, I know it doesn't compare. Having your husband shut you out must be incredibly difficult."

Jeneen nodded, and the tears that had pooled in her eyes spilled over onto her cheeks. Breanna grabbed a tissue from the nearby desk and handed it to her.

"I know Steve would be glad to come over and try to talk to Chet," she offered, "but I imagine Chet wouldn't be too receptive to that." She sighed. "I just wish they knew each other better."

"Me too." Jeneen used the tissue to pat her cheeks dry. "In the meantime, if you two would just please pray for him . . . for us." She swallowed a sob. "I would so appreciate it."

Breanna reached out and pulled her friend into an embrace. "Of course I will. And let me offer a quick prayer for you now. All right?"

Jeneen nodded, and the two closed their eyes as Breanna prayed for wisdom for Jeneen, healing for Chet and their family, and peace in their home. When they opened their eyes, Breanna saw that one of the other mothers had come in with her little girl. Breanna and the other mom, whose name was Lily, exchanged smiles as the mother turned to sign in her child, and Jeneen thanked Breanna and headed out the door.

"That was so nice of you," Lily said.

Breanna frowned. "Excuse me?"

Lily smiled. "I heard a little of the prayer you were saying when I came in. I can't tell you what it means to me to know you care enough about these children and their families that you would actually pray for them."

Breanna felt her cheeks warm. "I . . . I appreciate your saying that. Because this isn't a Christian school, I try not to offend anyone by being overt about my faith. But I will admit to praying for many of you regularly."

"That's absolutely wonderful." Lily was nearly beaming now as she watched her daughter scamper off to play. She turned her attention back to Breanna. "My husband and I weren't raised with any sort of religion, and even now we seldom attend church unless it's to drop in for an occasional Christmas or Easter service. So I suppose it's that much more special to know that the lady who runs our daughter's preschool prays for us." She shook her head. "It's amazing, actually. Now that I think about it, I don't know anyone else who prays for us. Thank you for doing that. It means a lot."

Breanna's heart warmed at Lily's words. She recalled her recent misgivings about founding a secular school rather than a Christian one, and Lily's words settled over her heart like a comforting blanket.

"It's truly my privilege and pleasure, Lily. And please, feel free to ask me for specific prayers anytime you wish."

Lily smiled and nodded. "I will." Then she turned and walked out the door, leaving Breanna with tears of joy stinging her eyes.

IT WAS mid-morning before Chet awoke, groaning as he pulled himself from a deep sleep. He glanced at the clock beside his bed and groaned again. No doubt Jeneen had given up on him as a babysitter and taken Kevin to preschool instead.

She's probably right, he thought as he headed for the bathroom. *I'm no good as a husband or a father, and I'm sure not any good at being a provider. And what else is there?*

Skipping a shower, he threw on his clothes from the day before and headed barefoot for the kitchen. The first thing that greeted him was a note propped up on the counter. With a sigh, he opened it.

"Chet, I decided to take Kevin to school today so you could sleep in. Also, if you get a call about work, you won't have to worry about getting him to school first. See you this evening."

No "love, Jeneen"? He snorted. *What a surprise. Who's going to love a loser like me? But she didn't have to worry about me getting a call to come in to work. That doesn't look like it's going to happen any time soon—if ever.*

He threw the note back on the counter and crossed the kitchen to pour what was left of the coffee into a mug. He took a sip then shrugged his shoulders. *Cold. Oh well, who cares?*

Chet padded into the family room and took in the decorated Christmas tree. *Gotta admit, it looks good—no thanks to me.*

He grabbed the remote and sank down onto the couch. Taking another sip of cold coffee, he turned on the TV and prepared to channel surf until he found something worth watching. He was surprised when the face of a well-known preacher filled the screen.

"The Bible tells us that all have sinned; not one of us is good enough to come into God's holy presence." Chet's hand froze on the remote as the older man seemed to look straight into his eyes. "But it also tells us that it isn't God's will for any of us to perish; He wants everyone to repent and come to Him. And because of Jesus' sacrifice at Calvary, we can do that."

Chet's heart raced as the man's words dredged up childhood memories of sitting in church with his mother and attending Sunday school regularly. He'd known all those verses by heart once. How had he let them slip away?

As the preacher went on to talk about the need to repent, to turn away from sin and toward God, his thoughts drifted back to Mike's memorial service. He sensed that the peace he'd seen in Dani somehow tied in to the verses and teaching he'd learned as a child. Was God somehow trying to speak to Him, to remind him of the great truths he had once known and then rejected?

Chet shook his head and pushed the thoughts from his mind. Then he angrily punched the channel selection button, exchanging the preacher's words for an ad about a certain fabric softener that smelled so good you'd want to bury your nose in the clean, fresh clothes.

Yeah, right. Chet took another slug of coffee. *At least we know what they say about the fabric softener isn't true. But what about what that preacher's saying? How could so many people be suckered into buying what he's selling? Even my own mom and my wife—and no doubt my son now, too—have convinced themselves it's true. What a bunch of hype.*

The fabric softener commercial came to an end, and contestants on a game show filled the screen. *A bunch of idiots doing ridiculous things to try to win some money. But hey, why not? They have a better chance of becoming a millionaire on that stupid show than I do of getting a job and collecting a regular paycheck so I can take care of my family.*

He sipped his coffee until the show ended. Then he returned to the kitchen, where he poked around in the fridge until he found a couple pieces of very old chicken. He sniffed it and shrugged. *Seems OK to me.*

Considering whether or not to make a fresh pot of coffee, he finally decided against it and reopened the refrigerator. He'd noticed a couple cans of beer on the bottom shelf, and that sounded like a great way to wash down leftover chicken.

With his two stale drumsticks and two cold beers in hand, he returned to the family room, plunked down onto the sofa once again, and resumed his channel surfing. It was going to be a long day, and he had no idea how he was going to fill the time. But one thing he knew for certain: he wasn't about to give in to Jeneen's nagging and call about that support group. If that's what his life had come to, there really wasn't much point in going on.

CHAPTER 29

Breanna was exhausted. Not only were they short-handed because of Dani being out all week and the inability to get a substitute at the last minute, but Breanna had been inundated with questions and concerns from parents who had read her note about Dani's recent loss.

Thank goodness this day is just about over, she thought as she waved goodbye to another parent who'd come to pick up a child. Only a handful of children remained, including Kevin. She glanced at her watch. It wouldn't be long now until she could lock up for the day and take Ryan home. Steve had said he'd be home early today and would have dinner ready when she got there. She smiled at the thought.

"Mommy!" Kevin's voice pulled her from her thoughts, and she turned to see the curly-haired blond racing toward his mother. Breanna followed closely behind, smiling at Jeneen as she approached.

"Long day?" Breanna asked.

Jeneen nodded. "Yes, and I'm so sorry to be running late again. I should have called. I know you're as anxious to get home as we all are."

A shadow flickered across Jeneen's face, as if the reality of her words had suddenly hit her. Breanna sensed her friend had mixed emotions about going home and what she would have to deal with when she got there.

"Don't worry about it," she said, laying a hand on Jeneen's arm as Kevin stood with arms wrapped around his mother's legs, gazing up at her face. No doubt the reason he was anxious to leave Sun Valley and go home had to do with the fact that both James and Mark had left early that day.

"Seriously," Breanna continued, "it's not a problem. I'll be here for another half-hour or so anyway."

Jeneen nodded as she glanced around the room. "So how are the kids doing with Dani's absence? Have many of the parents responded to your note?"

"Quite a few actually. Most wanted advice on how best to tell a child about something like this. How many of them actually followed through I don't know." She sighed. "Dani will be back on Monday, so we'll see how everyone reacts then."

Breanna squeezed Jeneen's arm before removing her hand. "So how did your day go? You doing all right?"

Jeneen bent down to pick up Kevin. "Better," she said, refocusing on Breanna. "I really appreciate you taking the time to pray with me."

"Any time." Breanna smiled at the perky little boy in Jeneen's arms. "And how about you, young man? Did you have a good day today?"

Kevin nodded, though not as vigorously as usual. "I played with James and Mark, but then they went home."

"Yes, they left early today, didn't they?" She reached out and patted the boy's shoulder. "But they'll be back tomorrow."

Kevin's contagious grin and dancing eyes returned. "Yay!" He turned to his mother. "Can I come to school and play with James and Mark tomorrow? Please, Mom?"

Jeneen lifted her eyebrows. "Unless your dad has something special planned for you for tomorrow, I don't see why not. But if he does, I think you should stay home and play with him instead, don't you?"

For a split second the boy looked torn, but then he nodded. "Daddy gets sad sometimes. I'll stay home with him."

Jeneen's eyes filled with tears, and Breanna felt her own heart tug at the child's comment. Out of the mouths of babes, indeed!

"Well, we'd better get going," Jeneen said. "We'll most likely see you in the morning, but if not, you'll know why."

Breanna nodded and watched the mother and child exit the building. Then she sighed and turned back to the few remaining students, wondering how many of them had situations at home that might force them to abandon their childlike innocence far too soon. Though she might not be free to share about the Lord's love for them, she could pray for them regularly—and she would

JENEEN'S HEART raced as she pulled into the garage and parked her car next to Chet's truck. What would she find when she went into the house? Would he be in a good mood or a bad one? Would he be kind and caring as he was when she had a cold? Or would he be sullen and withdrawn, refusing to speak to her, possibly already sleeping to avoid any chance at conversation?

She sighed and walked inside with Kevin, who immediately raced into the family room when he heard the sound of the TV.

Jeneen set down the bag of groceries she'd picked up on the way home. Fish sticks, rice, and peas would have to do for tonight. Kevin liked it, even if she and Chet weren't crazy about it, and it was quick and easy. Throw in a quick salad, and at least the meal would be relatively healthy.

The sound of her husband and son laughing made her heart soar. Maybe Chet was in a good mood after all.

She took a chance and headed for the family room, stopping in the doorway when she saw the mess that greeted her. A couple of empty beer cans grabbed her attention first, but then she saw an empty chip bag, an almost empty cookie package, and chicken bones on a paper plate.

Jeneen sighed. It could have been worse. At least she knew he wasn't drunk since the only alcohol that had been in the house when she left that morning were the two beers in the fridge. He'd obviously found those, but from the looks of his unshaven face, matted hair, and rumpled pj's, he hadn't bothered to go to the store for more.

Forcing a smile, she stepped into the room just as Chet and Kevin erupted in another fit of giggles.

"Sounds like you two are having a great time. Care to let me in on your joke?"

Both her husband and son turned their faces in her direction. Chet's expression was noncommittal, but Kevin jumped right in.

"It's not a joke, Mom," he explained. "We were talking about our favorite cartoon." He pointed to the TV, which now featured a colorful animated show. "See? Daddy just put it on for me."

"That was very nice of Daddy," Jeneen said, trying to engage Chet with her eyes. "So are you two hungry?"

"I'm starved!" Kevin exclaimed before turning to his father. "We're having fish sticks, Daddy. We got it on the way home."

Chet lifted his eyebrows in her direction before turning back to his son. "One of your favorites, right?" He smiled and winked. "Next to peanut butter."

Kevin laughed again. "Yep. I love peanut butter, but fish sticks are almost as good. What did you eat for lunch today, Daddy?"

Chet glanced at the remains of his day's feast, pointing to it as he spoke. "You're looking at it. Nothing very good, I'm afraid."

"You should have had a peanut-butter sandwich, Daddy."

Chet shrugged. "You weren't here to make it for me."

"I'll make it for you tomorrow," Kevin promised. "I can stay home with you if you want."

Chet nodded and tousled Kevin's hair. "I'd like that. Thanks, buddy."

Her two boys turned their attention back to the antics of the cartoon characters on the screen, and Jeneen sighed and made her way back to the kitchen to make a quick dinner. *At least Kevin will like it,* she thought.

ONCE AGAIN Chet berated himself for being so awful to Jeneen, but sometimes he didn't seem able to stop himself. It was easier with Kevin. The boy was young and good-natured and didn't demand anything of him. In fact, he seemed to appreciate the smallest thing Chet did for him.

Jeneen, on the other hand, somehow managed to bring every conversation around to his need for counseling or a support group. He'd come to the point where he figured she was probably right that he had PTSD, but he couldn't bring himself to tell her that, and he sure didn't want to sit around in a group of losers and misfits and discuss his "issues."

Issues. I hate that word, he thought as he lay in bed later that night, going over the events of the day and pretending to be asleep so he and Jeneen wouldn't end up rehashing the same conversation. *Why can't she just lay off and let me deal with this on my own? I don't need a group of people to tell me I'm messed up. I already know that.*

A muffled sob caught his attention, and he very nearly turned over to take his wife in his arms. But he knew he was the cause of her pain, and that knowledge kept him firmly in place.

Why does she even put up with me? Why doesn't she just take Kevin and leave and get it over with? Then she could be happy again, and I could just go fade away somewhere . . . .

The thought brought the hot sting of tears to his eyes, but still determined not to alert Jeneen that he was awake, he resisted the urge to brush them away. *Why, God? Why did You let this happen to us? Maybe I deserve it, but Jeneen and Kevin don't. Help them, God, please!*

The realization that he had prayed for the first time in years washed over him, and he could no longer hold back the tears. With a deep groan, he sobbed aloud and let the tears flow, bracing himself for the barrage of words that was bound to come.

But his wife said nothing. Instead she came and pressed up against his back and put her arm over him. Then she held him tight as, wordlessly, they cried together.

CHAPTER 30

hristmas was just a week away now, and Chet still hadn't received any calls to go to work. Jeneen sighed as she prepared a quick breakfast for the three of them. It was Friday; tomorrow they could all sleep in, and Chet had volunteered to keep an eye on Kevin so she could get some last-minute shopping done. He'd also offered to drop off Kevin at Sun Valley that morning so he could see his friends one more time before the weekend. With her busy schedule breathing down her neck, Jeneen had readily agreed.

She smiled as she thought of the recently improved atmosphere in their home. Since the night she and Chet had cried together, the tension between them had lessened. Chet had even reached out to her on occasion, giving her hope that they were at last back on the right track, even though they admittedly still had a long way to go.

She poured three glasses of orange juice and finished setting the table. As grateful as she was for Chet's efforts, she was concerned that he had yet to make any moves toward accompanying her and Kevin to church or getting in touch with a support group. It was obvious his wall had yet to come down, though she prayed it was at least crumbling around the edges.

Jeneen looked up when she heard Kevin thundering down the hallway. "I'm going to school today," he announced as he exploded into the room. "Daddy's taking me so I can play with James and Mark."

She smiled. "So I heard. That's wonderful. I also heard you running in the hallway." She raised her eyebrows. "Anything to say about that?"

His smile faded slightly. "Sorry," he mumbled. "I'm not supposed to run in the house." His face lit up again. "But I'm excited."

Jeneen laughed. "I noticed. Are you ready for some cereal and juice?"

He nodded vigorously. "Yep. I'm starved!"

Jeneen laughed again as Chet came into the room. She was so pleased to see him freshly showered and in clean clothes again. He'd even shaved. And for the first time in months, he didn't seem stressed about money. She just hoped the good mood would last.

He walked up to her and planted a kiss on her cheek. "Morning. I understand our son is starved. I'm just about there myself."

Their eyes met, and they shared a smile that warmed Jeneen's heart. "Hope you don't mind cereal. I didn't have much time this morning."

"No problem. Tomorrow's Saturday, and since you'll be fighting the crowds at the mall all day, it'll be my turn to cook." He looked at Kevin. "I'm thinking pancakes and scrambled eggs and bacon for breakfast. Want to help?"

Kevin's blue eyes went wide as his face lit up. "Yes! Can we do it today?"

Chet laughed and shook his head. "No, buddy, not today. Your mom has to get to work, and I'm taking you to school, remember? But tomorrow for sure. I promise."

Jeneen and Chet took their seats, and she offered up a brief prayer of thanks for their food. She knew Kevin bowed his head with her when she prayed, but Chet did not. He waited patiently until she finished, but he simply chose not to participate.

Oh well, at least he doesn't seem to mind that Kevin and I pray, she thought, pouring milk on her cereal. *Maybe one of these days . . .*

CHET PULLED into the Sun Valley parking lot and checked to be sure Kevin's jacket was zipped before getting him out of the truck. The weather had turned cool, and it looked like rain.

"Be sure and wear that if you play outside," Chet said.

Kevin nodded, and Chet knew the boy was anxious to get out on the playground with his friends.

They headed inside, and before Chet got his son signed in, the boy had hugged him around the knees, tossed off a quick, "See you later, Dad," and made a beeline for the back-door that would take him out onto the playground.

Chet smiled and shook his head. If only he had half of his child's energy.

"Hi, Chet. How are you this morning?"

He lifted his head and found himself looking into Breanna's green eyes. Her smile was warm, contagious, and he returned it without thinking.

"I'm fine," he answered. "How about you and the family?"

"We're doing well. Looking forward to Christmas, though I admit I'll be glad when all the hoopla that precedes it settles down and we can concentrate on what it's really about."

Though he knew it wasn't a personal dig, he suddenly felt uncomfortable nevertheless. He imagined it was because he hadn't thought much lately about the real meaning of Christmas.

He cleared his throat. "Yeah, me too. Well, I'd better get going."

He turned to leave then remembered he had Kevin's favorite Matchbox car in his pocket. The boy had told him it was for show-and-tell that day. He pulled it from his pocket and turned around.

"This is Kevin's show-and-tell toy today. I forgot to give it to him. Would you mind?"

"Of course not," Breanna answered. "But you're welcome to take it outside to him yourself if you're not in a hurry."

A hurry for what? No time-clock punching scheduled for my day. "Sure. Thanks. I'd like that."

He headed for the back door and was about to step outside on the playground when he caught sight of a little boy sitting alone in the corner of the room near the doorway. Chet could tell by the child's hunched shoulders and bowed head that it was Ryan, and his heart twisted inside him.

Poor kid. What's he been through already in his short life? Worse yet, what has he got to look forward to if he doesn't get over his past?

The words echoed in his heart as Ryan lifted his head and looked straight at him, almost as if he'd know Chet would be there. Once again, their eyes connected as they had the previous time across the table, and Chet thought he saw a message in the child's dark eyes.

He nodded, and Ryan quickly stuck his thumb in his mouth and ducked his head. Chet took a shaky breath and headed outside to find his son.

DANI SHARED playground duty with one other aides that morning, and she wasn't surprised to see Kevin burst through the door and dash toward the slide. James hadn't arrived yet, but Mark was already there. They greeted one another excitedly and immediately began zipping up and down the slide nonstop.

Then she spotted Kevin's dad, Chet, heading toward the boys. She watched him hand something to his son, say hello to Mark, and then turn and head back toward the door that led inside.

She intercepted him halfway there. "Hello, Mr. Mason. Nice to see you again."

Dani watched closely as the man's look of puzzlement turned to recognition. "Oh, yes . . . Dani, isn't it?"

She nodded. "How are you?"

His expression changed again, and she realized he had just remembered what happened to Mike. That knowledge obviously made him uncomfortable.

"I'm . . . sorry," he said. "About your . . . your loss. Mike seemed like a . . . great guy."

She managed to speak past the lump in her throat. "He was. The best, actually."

Chet nodded, looking like he'd rather be anywhere but there on the playground with her.

"It's all right," she said. When he looked puzzled again, she added, "That you don't know what to say, I mean."

His shoulders relaxed visibly, and he cleared his throat. "Thanks. It's just that . . . he was so young. Like a lot of the guys we lost over in . . ."

His voice trailed off. "Anyway, I'm sorry, but I need to get going."

Chet's pained expression moved her. She laid a hand on his arm. "Really. It's all right. I'm hurting right now, but I'll see him again. That's what gets me through."

Sudden tears shimmered in Chet's eyes, and he nodded one last time before shaking off her hand and heading for the door.

CHAPTER 31

*C*het smiled as he stirred the pancake batter. He had no doubt that his son would be thrilled with breakfast that Saturday morning. Jeneen had snagged a cup of coffee before leaving more than an hour earlier, off on her quest to finish her Christmas shopping.

He was about to pour the first batch onto the griddle when the doorbell rang. Frowning, he set down the pancake batter and headed for the front door, trying to figure out who would be dropping by on Saturday morning.

He opened the door and smiled. His mother. Of course! Jeneen had told her on the phone the previous evening that she was going shopping and leaving the boys home to fend for themselves. Chet's only misgiving was that she'd opted to come and visit them instead of accompanying Jeneen on her shopping venture.

"Hey, Mom," he said, warily pushing the screen door open. "This is a nice surprise."

She smiled as she stepped inside and returned his hug before pulling away to remove her jacket. "It's chilly out there this morning, but when Jeneen told me my two favorite guys would be home alone today, I decided to pop over and see what you two are up to—especially since I finished the last of my own Christmas shopping a few days ago."

Chet accepted her explanation about why she hadn't accompanied Jeneen, though he knew there was more to it. Telling himself her motives weren't important, he took her jacket and hung it in the coat closet in the entryway then escorted her into the kitchen.

"We're not up to much, really—at least Kevin isn't. I'm making his favorite breakfast—pancakes, scrambled eggs, and bacon. After that, we don't have any plans."

Celia smiled. "Kevin isn't the only one who loves pancakes, eggs, and bacon. I'm glad all I had was a cup of coffee before I came over. I believe I'll invite myself to join you."

Chet chuckled. "You know you're always welcome, Mom—anytime."

"I do know that, son." She opened the cupboard and grabbed some plates then placed them on the table before returning to the silverware drawer for knives and forks. "And it's been far too long since we've had alone time. Thanksgiving was lovely, of course, but we were inundated with other people and their conversations. It will be nice for the three of us to be together today without outside interruptions."

Chet nodded, pleased at her words as he watched the batter bubble on the griddle. "I know what you mean. Thanksgiving was overwhelming."

Celia faced him with a carton of orange juice in her hands. "I heard that young man who was here—Mike, wasn't it?—had a terrible accident and went home to be with the Lord." She shook her head and sighed. "We can be grateful we know where he is and we'll see him again one day, but it must be so very hard on the young lady who was here with him. They seemed to be heading for a permanent relationship."

"You're right," Chet agreed, flipping the pancakes. "I saw Dani at the preschool yesterday when I dropped Kevin off. It's obvious she's heartbroken, but she seemed to have a real peace about it all."

Celia began filling three glasses with juice. "Yes, I can imagine that. They both seemed like strong believers. I know that doesn't take away our pain, but it certainly does enable us to get through it with God's help, knowing that something far better lies ahead."

Chet scooped the first of the pancakes from the griddle onto a plate. Not wanting to pursue the conversation further, he cleared his throat. "Mom, would you like to go wake Kevin? Let him know what we're having for breakfast, and he'll no doubt bounce out of bed without a problem."

Celia smiled. "Glad to. He's such a cheerful little boy, so different from the other child that was here at Thanksgiving. Ryan, was it? Poor little guy."

She headed for the hallway, and Chet heaved a sigh of relief. He should know better than to get into a discussion with his mom about anything even remotely related to religion. If he hadn't steered her in another direction, she would have made every effort to bring the discussion around to a personal level, reminding him how he'd been raised in church and once made a profession of faith.

He frowned as he poured another batch of pancakes onto the griddle, finding himself asking the very questions his mother no doubt would have done if he'd let her. What had happened to that trusting boy who once loved Jesus? Where had his faith gone, and why had he allowed it to slip away? The biggest question was one that had haunted him quite a bit the past few days: Was it possible to get it back?

Laughter from his mother and son drew near, and he pushed the questions from his mind as he placed the butter and syrup on the table. *Enough heavy thoughts for now. Time to enjoy two of the three people who matter most in my life.* Mike's death had been a reminder he couldn't take anyone's presence for granted, but he couldn't imagine going on without his mother or son . . . or Jeneen.

IT HAD taken Jeneen nearly fifteen minutes to snag a parking place at the mall. *Everybody and his brother must be here today,* she thought, locking her car before heading for the nearest entrance. *Oh well, that's what I get for putting this off until the last minute.*

It was no better inside. Crowds pushed past in each direction, and the line to see Santa stretched out farther than she'd ever seen it. Cranky and impatient children whined and fussed, while parents peered anxiously toward the front of the line.

Jeneen smiled. She was grateful that Chet had taken Kevin for his annual Santa visit earlier in the week. She couldn't imagine standing in line with her energetic three-year-old today.

I'm so glad I already ordered a big fruit basket for Mom and Pete. It should be delivered to them in the next couple of days. She sighed. *I should feel bad that they aren't coming to join us for Christmas, but I'm actually relieved. And the important thing is that I at least invited them. Maybe next year . . .*

She had no trouble finding a couple of last-minute items for Kevin and a lovely sweater for her mother-in-law, but she was stumped for ideas for Chet. She'd never had any problem putting together packages for him when he was overseas—not just for Christmas but throughout the year. But now that he was home, it was much more difficult.

What would he like? There was a time he'd enjoyed fishing, but he hadn't gone once since he'd been back. She decided she'd suggest that he take Kevin fishing. Maybe that would rekindle Chet's interest in a healthy activity. Lately, all he seemed to want to do is hang around the house and watch TV or sleep.

Determined to push him out of that habit and into something he would surely enjoy again, she headed for a sporting goods store. Maybe she'd find a gift that would work for both father and son.

It didn't take long to find matching hats with the emblem of a jumping fish on a line. She knew Kevin would love his; she hoped Chet would be at least half as enthusiastic.

She headed out of the sporting goods store and back into the crowded mall. Smells of popcorn and gooey cinnamon rolls beckoned her toward the food court, but before she could respond, she sensed God steering her elsewhere.

A Bible? She frowned. *For Chet? But Lord, he doesn't even want to go to church with us.*

The nudging continued, so she gave in and aimed for the Christian bookstore. Even as she browsed the numerous versions, she wondered how Chet would respond to such a gift. Would he be offended, or might he actually appreciate it?

Leave that to Me.

The silent words were clear as she picked up a Bible aimed at men. She opened it and glanced through it. Every few pages the Scriptures were interspersed with a brief devotional thought, all written by men and directed to men. Would it be too much? *Father, is this the one?*

Peace flowed over her like warm honey, and she carried the Bible to the front. Only two people in line ahead of her. In less than ten minutes, she'd laid the Bible in its box on the counter.

A cheerful young woman smiled at her. "Would you like it giftwrapped? No charge."

She hadn't thought of that, but nodded in response. "Yes, please." She watched as the woman turned and placed the box on a table filled with paper and bows. "Wait!" Jeneen was almost surprised to realize she'd spoken aloud.

The woman turned back and raised her eyebrows. "Yes?"

Jeneen felt her cheeks warm, but she took a deep breath and spoke the rest of her sudden thought. "This is for my husband, and I'd like it engraved with his name before you wrap it."

The young woman smiled again. "Of course. Can you write his name down for me? I'll need a little time to get it done, as we have a couple ahead of you." She glanced at her watch and then back at Jeneen. "Thirty minutes? If you can come back then, I can have it engraved and wrapped and waiting for you."

Jeneen nodded as she printed Chet's name on the paper the clerk had laid in front of her. "That would be great. Thank you so much."

Then she headed out of the store and followed her nose toward the delicious smells that beckoned her.

BREANNA HAD slept in longer than she'd expected that Saturday. When she finally joined her husband and son in the kitchen, she smiled at the array of fruits and muffins on the table.

"Wow, my two men have really outdone themselves," she said, smiling up at Steve as he gave her a welcoming hug and kiss. Then she glanced at Ryan, who sat quietly in his chair at the table, eyes downcast as he ate a banana.

"Good morning, Ryan," she said. "Did you help Daddy make this wonderful breakfast?"

The three-year-old looked up briefly and nodded, then dropped his eyes again and continued to eat his breakfast.

Her heart warmed. They were making progress, since there was a time not long ago that Ryan wouldn't even meet her eyes with his own.

She dropped a quick kiss on her son's head and then sat down next to him. Steve poured her a cup of coffee—with double cream, just the way she liked it—and then took his seat as well.

Breanna offered a silent word of thanks to her husband and son. Then she looked up and smiled. "OK, you two, I'd like to know what's going on here. Not only did I get to sleep late, but then I come out here and find a wonderful breakfast waiting for me. So tell me the truth: did Santa come early this year?"

The slight chuckle that came from Ryan's still bowed head was the closest thing to laughter that she'd heard from her beloved son, and her heart soared. She looked at Steve and saw a glisten in his dark eyes as he smiled and nodded.

Oh, Lord, thank You! she prayed silently. *You are so faithful!*

"Well," Steve said, "I think I can assure you that Santa did not come early. Nope, it was just Ryan and me who decided to let you get some extra sleep while we made breakfast. I could never have done it without his help."

Ryan's head lifted again, and Breanna was certain she saw the trace of a smile turn his lips upward. This was truly turning into a wonderful day, and she couldn't help but believe it would only get better between now and Christmas.

CHAPTER 32

Breanna opened the preschool on Monday morning and carried the still sleeping Ryan to one of the cots, where she covered him before heading back for the office. She knew attendance would be up through the holidays because so many children were out of school and needed a place to stay while their parents were at work. As a result, she'd brought in a couple of extra aides to help. Dani, of course, was among them, though Breanna had offered to give her the week off if she needed it.

"Oh, no, not at all," she'd objected. "I'm not foolish enough to think I can get through Christmas without a serious meltdown unless I stay busy and focused. Seriously, I'd like all the hours you can give me. My parents are arriving the day after Christmas to spend a few days with me—to sort of celebrate a late Christmas together—so I'd like some extra time off that week if possible."

Breanna had happily obliged, reminding herself to spend extra time in prayer for the girl. This had to be an unbelievably difficult time for her, and she was glad she had family coming to be with her.

With that thought still on her mind, she spotted Dani in the kitchen, preparing the morning snack. *Good timing,* she thought as she joined the girl at the counter.

"Looks like you're getting a good start on the busy day," she observed, grabbing a second pitcher of juice and helping Dani fill the paper cups halfway.

Dani nodded, her ponytail bouncing slightly. "You said there'd probably be extra kids this week, so I thought I'd get started on the snack before they all showed up."

"Good planning." Breanna paused and studied the lovely young woman who wore her sadness with grace. "I've been thinking about something," she said at last.

"I assume you're planning to attend Christmas Eve service at church, right?"

Dani glanced at her and nodded. "Absolutely. Wouldn't miss it."

Breanna smiled. "I thought as much. Steve and I—and Ryan too, of course—will be there, so why not come home with us afterward? I've invited Jeneen and Chet and Kevin. Surprisingly, Jeneen said Chet agreed, so we're all gathering at our house after church, even Chet's mother. Steve will read the Christmas story from the Bible, and I'm planning to make some traditional Wassail and cookies. It's something Steve and I have done since we got married, and we thought it would be nice to include some of our extended family this year." She laid her hand on Dani's arm. "I'm so glad you'll be with us."

Dani's brown eyes watered, and Breanna could tell she was struggling for an answer. "I am to," she said at last. "Truly I am. As much as I love the Lord and want to celebrate and honor Him that evening, I wasn't sure how I was going to get through it—until now."

She reached for Breanna, who gladly pulled her into a tight hug.

KEVIN HAD been even more excitable and energetic than usual throughout the day. Now it was nearly time to leave for the Christmas Eve service.

Jeneen's stomach tightened at the thought that had nagged her all day. *Give Chet his Bible now.* She knew it was God, so it had to be the right thing to do, but she dreaded Chet's reaction, especially since she'd planned to ask him to come to church with them that evening.

She cleaned off the kitchen table after the light supper they'd all shared. The clock was ticking, and they'd have to leave soon or be late for the service. *Oh Father, I want to be obedient, but he's going to feel overwhelmed if I invite him* to church and give him the Bible too. *What should I do? How do I handle this?*

The silent response was yet loud and clear, and it nearly knocked her to her knees.

Leave that to me. Do as I told you, and give him his Bible now.

Obediently, Jeneen dried her hands and hung up the dishtowel then made her way to the linen closet where she'd done her best to hide their Christmas gifts. She'd gotten nice wrapping for Chet's Bible and placed this gift with the other presents, planning to put them all under the tree after Kevin went to bed.

She reached into the closet and pulled out the gift-wrapped package she'd brought home from the mall, took a deep breath, and carried it to their bedroom where she imagined Chet would be. He obviously knew she and Kevin were headed to church soon, so the logical place for him to be was lying on the bed watching TV, rather than being in the kitchen or family room where Kevin would certainly invite him to come with them.

Surprisingly Chet wasn't watching TV but had instead just stepped out of the shower. Towel-drying his hair, another towel wrapped around his waist, he stepped out of the bathroom just as she entered the bedroom.

"Good. I'm glad you're here," he said, walking to the closet and sliding the door open. "You can help me pick out what I should wear."

She frowned, laid the wrapped gift down on the bed, and walked toward the closet to join him. "What you should wear for what? Are you going somewhere?"

Pawing through the shirts hanging in front of him, Chet said, "This is Christmas Eve, and you and Kevin are going to church, right?"

Jeneen lifted her eyebrows. Where was this headed? "Yes, but . . ."

He stopped going through shirts and looked at her. "I thought maybe I'd . . . come along. If that's all right, of course."

Jeneen felt her eyes widen. "If it's all right?" She swallowed. "There's nothing we'd like better. But I just thought—"

"You thought I'd be staying home, watching TV and feeling sorry for myself. Maybe even drowning my sorrows in a six-pack."

She swallowed, her cheeks growing hot. "Oh, no, I didn't think—"

His smile was tentative, but it warmed Jeneen's heart. "It doesn't matter what you thought. Really. And I don't blame you. I haven't exactly been easy to live with lately." He shrugged. "But it's Christmas Eve, and since we're picking Mom up after the service and going over to your friends' place, I figured it'd be easier if you didn't have to stop by here and pick me up too. So . . . OK with you?"

Hot tears pricked her eyelids, and she nodded. "More than OK," she managed to choke out before leaning her head against his chest as he pulled her into his arms.

"I'm going to try harder," Chet murmured, his chin resting on top of her head. "I can't promise I won't still have some serious down times, but I really am going to try. And maybe going to church with you and Kevin tonight is a good place to start."

She nodded and pulled back. "It's a wonderful place to start," she said, resisting the urge to mention his need for a support group and counseling. "Thank you, Chet."

His smile was broader this time as he bent down to kiss her.

Give him his Bible.

She cleared her throat. "I have something for you."

He lifted his eyebrows. "A present? I thought we were going to wait and open them with Kevin in the morning."

"The other gifts, yes." She smiled up at him. "But this one came with special instructions about giving it to you tonight—now."

Chet shrugged. "OK. You've got my curiosity up anyway. So where is it?" His glance darted toward the bed. "Would that be it over there?"

Still smiling, she took his hand and led him to the bed. They sat down on the edge together. "Merry Christmas, my love," she said as she handed him the gift. Then she waited as he slowly opened it, careful to preserve the wrappings. Her heart was thrumming in her ears by the time he finally took the lid off the box.

He sat there, quietly, staring at the Bible, while Jeneen squeezed her fingernails into her palms. Would he like it? Would he become irritated or resentful and cancel his plans to go with them? Had she really heard from God at all, or had she just imagined it? If so, she'd probably made a huge mistake, and if Chet ended up back in a dark and depressed state, it would be all her fault.

At last he lifted his head and turned to look at her. His brown eyes were wet. "It's beautiful," he said, his voice husky with emotion. "I haven't really had a Bible of my own since I was kid. Mom got it for me, but I have no idea what happened to it." As he continued to hold his gift in one hand, he reached out with the other and took her hand. "I know it's OK to go to church without a Bible, but it's really nice to have one of my own again." She watched his Adam's apple slide up and then down again as he swallowed. Then he squeezed her hand and said, "It's the nicest gift I've received in a really long time—maybe ever. I just wish I had something as nice to give you."

Tears bit her eyes again as she reached up and laid her hand against his cheek. "You just did," she whispered.

JENEEN COULDN'T remember a time when she'd enjoyed the Christmas Eve service more than this night. They'd even swung by and picked up Chet's mom on the way to church, so the four of them had walked in together and were now squeezed into the middle of a pew.

She glanced at Celia to her left, and the woman quickly responded with a grin that Jeneen knew represented her excitement at having Chet with them at church. She nodded and smiled in return, sharing her mother-in-law's feelings.

Kevin sat to Jeneen's right, with Chet on his other side. She couldn't help but smile at the memory of Kevin's reaction when he'd first realized his dad was going to church with them. His dark eyes had nearly bulged from his head, and he'd let out a whoop that Jeneen imagined all the neighbors for miles around could hear. Then he'd thrown his arms around his dad's legs, until Chet picked him up and the boy transferred the hug to Chet's neck. Then he'd closed his eyes and squealed, "Thank You, Jesus. You are awesome!"

Chet and Jeneen had chuckled, and even now the memory brought a warm glow to Jeneen's heart. Kevin knew exactly where to give credit and thanks for this Christmas miracle. *And he was absolutely right that You are awesome, Lord!*

As they stood to their feet to begin singing the familiar carols of Christmas, Jeneen had to check herself yet again about not pushing Chet to get involved with a support group or men's group at church or . . .

She sighed. *When will I learn, Lord? You do this so much better than I. I never imagined Chet would be here with us tonight, yet here he is—singing right along with the rest of us. Is it too much to hope that—?*

An invisible hand of restraint stopped her mid-thought. She was trying to do it again—the job that only God can do. *I'm sorry, Father. Forgive me, please. Help me to leave my husband in Your nail-scarred hands. My responsibility is to love and respect him; help me with that as well, Lord—even when I don't feel like it or he doesn't seem in the least bit receptive.*

She continued to sing as she prayed. *You so faithfully brought him home safe and sound from Afghanistan, and now You've brought him here to stand beside his family, worshipping You and celebrating the Gift of Christmas. As Kevin said, You truly are awesome, Lord!*

A tug on her pant leg snagged her attention, and she looked down to see Kevin peering up at her, his face alight with joy. "Best Christmas ever," he whispered then gave her a thumbs-up.

Jeneen nearly laughed aloud but managed to squelch it in time. She couldn't hide her joy, though—nor did she want to. She ruffled her son's curls then looked up to see if her husband had noticed their exchange.

His eyes were straight ahead, fixed on the words on the screen. If he was aware of Kevin's words or gesture, he didn't indicate it.

The touch of a hand on her shoulder told her that perhaps her mother-in-law had noticed. She turned to look into the woman's dancing eyes and wide grin. Yes, Celia had most certainly noticed and obviously agreed.

Jeneen's favorite part of the Christmas Eve service was the lighting of the candles just before the closing song. As the pastor finished his short commentary on the birth of Christ based on the second chapter of Luke, the ushers made their way to the front of the church. Kevin held high the candle he'd received as they entered the sanctuary, and Jeneen wondered if it wouldn't be better to hold his candle for him now that it was about to be lit. She reached toward his hand to retrieve it, but Chet laid his hand on her arm before she could.

Jeneen looked up at him, surprised. His expression was gentle, but the shake of his head firm. "He'll be fine," he whispered, and Jeneen withdrew her hand.

He's right, she thought. *I need to quit hovering so much, especially when both his parents are right here to watch him.* She smiled as she remembered her father saying to her mother, "Stop being a helicopter mom. You hover too much." Apparently, she was more like her mother than she realized.

As the lights dimmed and they held their candles up to illuminate the room, she found herself once more on the verge of tears. But they were happy tears, tears that sprang from a heart that was at last hopeful and full of peace.

EPILOGUE

hough Chet still felt uncomfortable in crowds, he'd made it through the Christmas Eve service without any major issues. Now, as he pulled up and parked Jeneen's car in front of the Pritchards' home, he took a deep breath and shot a quick prayer heavenward.

Help me, Lord. I know I haven't been faithful lately, but I realized tonight that You welcomed my return. I have so far to go, so please guide me. And help me be kinder and more loving to others, especially my family.

They rang the doorbell and waited together for the door to open. When it did, they were welcomed by the entire Pritchard family, including Ryan who rested in his father's arms, his head buried in Steve's shoulder.

"Welcome! Come on in," Breanna said as they began to exchange hugs and greetings.

Chet noticed that Ryan didn't move, but he patted the boy on the back anyway. "Merry Christmas, buddy," he said.

The group had scarcely relocated to the family room to ooh and aah over the tree when the doorbell rang again. Chet frowned. He hadn't realized there would be other people too. He hoped it wasn't more than he could handle.

In a moment he heard a familiar voice and realized it belonged to the girl named Dani who worked at Sun Valley. How could she bear the pain of this season so soon after losing the man she had obviously cared for? His mind drifted back to the previous Christmas when he'd been overseas. Christmas had been the toughest time of all, even for those who didn't claim to share the Christian faith. Memories of loved ones tugged at their hearts, making the melancholy and loneliness almost unbearable. It had to be at least that bad for Dani now.

Breanna led Dani into the room, and Chet watched the girl with the blonde ponytail make the rounds, greeting each person by name, including Kevin and Ryan. Chet was pleasantly surprised when Ryan at least lifted his head at the sound of her voice, though the hint of a smile on his face was scarcely noticeable.

And then she stood in front of Chet to exchange a quick hug. "Merry Christmas. It's good to see you again."

He nodded. "You, too." He swallowed, knowing he should say something more but unable to find the words to do so. Her smile was genuine, he could tell, but sad, and it twisted his heart. He knew Dani was a believer, but he wondered if a personal faith could really be enough to overcome such a deep heartache. *If her faith is enough to get her past this, then anything's possible—even for me.*

"I think I'll light a fire in here," Steve announced, moving toward the fireplace with Ryan still in his arms.

Chet followed. "Can I help?"

Steve turned to him and smiled. "Trust me. This fire's so easy to light, even I can handle it." He flipped a switch and the fireplace sprang to life. He laughed. "We switched from wood to gas a couple years ago. I got too frustrated trying to get those logs to take hold."

Chet chuckled, and they both took a seat on the couch. Kevin quickly stepped up beside Steve and started talking to Ryan. "Want to go play?" he asked, holding up a Matchbox car in each hand. "I brought one for you."

Chet watched Ryan closely as the boy began to move in his father's arms.

"You want down?" Steve asked.

The boy's nod was nearly imperceptible, but it was enough. Steve set Ryan down on the floor next to Kevin. Ryan's eyes remained downcast as Kevin held out the two cars for the other boy to see.

"You can pick the one you want," Kevin offered.

Slowly Ryan reached toward the bright red car, ignoring the yellow truck.

Must like red, Chet thought, feeling as if he should cheer the boy on. *Come on, you can do it, buddy!*

As soon as the car was in his hand, Ryan turned and went to sit on the floor in the corner. Kevin followed, sitting down next to him, chattering and playing with his tiny truck as if Ryan were participating. But the wounded little boy just clutched the car in his hand and alternated between watching Kevin and staring at the floor.

Chet's heart ached. *Help him, Lord. He's so hurt. He needs You, and he needs other people too. Please open his heart!*

It wasn't long until all four women—Breanna, Jeneen, Celia, and Dani—returned to the room, bearing trays of hot chocolate and wassail, along with plates of decorated Christmas cookies.

Surely that will get the boy's attention, he thought, his gaze wandering from Ryan to the refreshments and back again. But Ryan didn't move.

Steve's voice interrupted his thoughts, and he turned to see Ryan's father standing in the middle of the room.

"We have a tradition in our family that we read the second chapter of Luke on Christmas Eve. You all probably heard it at church this evening, as did we, but I'd like to read it again. Then we'll dig into our treats and enjoy each other's company."

Chet saw no problem with that. In fact, he'd enjoyed listening to the pastor read the once-familiar story at the service that evening. *There was a time I knew those verses by heart, but it's been a long time.*

He settled back against the couch cushion and listened as Steve began to read.

"And it came to pass in those days . . ."

Chet glanced at Kevin and was relieved to see the boy had grown quiet and seemed to be listening intently.

"And she brought forth her firstborn Son, and wrapped Him in swaddling cloths, and laid Him in a manger . . . ."

When Ryan stood up, Chet had trouble concentrating on Steve's words. This was one of the few times he'd seen the child initiate something on his own. What did he have in mind?

"And behold, an angel of the Lord stood before them, and the glory of the Lord shone around them, and they were greatly afraid . . . ."

Ryan, head bowed, crossed the room until he stood only a couple of feet in front of Chet. Chet felt his heart race. Should he reach out to the boy somehow?

He glanced around the room. Steve still stood in the same place, reading from Scripture but occasionally peeking at his son. Everyone else's eyes were fixed on Ryan.

The boy stuck his thumb in his mouth and turned away from Chet, breaking Chet's hope that Ryan was going to come to him. Then the child took a tiny, tentative step backward. One . . . and then another . . .

"Do not be afraid, for behold, I bring you good tidings of great joy which will be to all people . . . ."

Ryan was nearly touching Chet's knees now. Should he reach out to him?

He cast a questioning glance at the others in the room, but they looked as surprised as he was.

One more step, and the connection had been made—light as a feather, but at least they were touching.

I have to do something. I can't just ignore him.

This time he looked straight at Steve, who had stopped reading for a moment. His eyes were wide, but when they met with Chet's, he nodded.

Chet carefully reached out with one arm until Ryan could see his hand. Then everything seemed to stop as they waited.

After a few silent seconds, Ryan took Chet's large hand in both of his tiny ones. The child's slight tremor brought tears to Chet's eyes, and he didn't even try to blink them back. Instead he continued to wait as Steve returned to reading.

"... And suddenly there was with the angel a multitude of the heavenly host praising God and saying: Glory to God in the highest, And on earth peace, goodwill toward men!"

It was all Chet could do not to shout amen. He remained perfectly still and silent as Steve completed his reading and closed his Bible.

It was then that Ryan turned toward Chet, removed his thumb from his mouth, and climbed up onto his lap. Then he laid his head against the man's chest.

Kevin was the first to respond. He came to stand in front of Chet and Ryan and declared in a hushed tone, "I think it's a Christmas miracle."

His words enabled the others to join in, each of them commenting on the event while trying not to overwhelm the little boy in Chet's lap.

"I've only seen him do that two other times," Steve said. "Once with Breanna and once with me, but it wasn't until he'd been with us for more than a year."

"Do you mean he came to you and Breanna in a similar way?" Jeneen asked. "Backing up to you?"

Breanna nodded. "Yes. It's not uncommon for children with Attachment Disorder—usually children who were taken from their primary caregivers at a very young age—to refuse to touch other people. They're afraid to form a connection because they fear losing yet another caregiver. Because Ryan lost his mother at such a young age and was then taken away from everything familiar to him before coming to live with us, he's been diagnosed with the disorder. One of the things our case-worker told us to watch for was Ryan coming to a point that he would finally approach us on his own. She also said it might very well be by backing up to us."

She shook her head. "That's exactly how Ryan initially bonded with Steve and me, but it never occurred to me that he might do the same with someone else."

"Maybe he felt some sort of connection with Chet," Steve suggested. "They say people with PTSD and Attachment Disorder have a lot in common."

Chet could tell the moment the words left Steve's mouth that he wished he could pull them back.

"It's all right," Chet assured him. "I've been resisting the diagnosis of PTSD, but I know now that's what I have. I'll be starting counseling soon after the first of the year. And I plan to get involved in a support group right away." He looked at Jeneen, who sat beside him, unmoving. "And I also plan to renew my relationship with God. That's the only way I'll ever really get better and become the man my family needs me to be."

The tears that had pooled in Jeneen's eyes spilled over onto her cheeks, but once again it was Kevin who reeled the conversation back in.

"What an awesome day!" he declared, his face shining. "I *love* Christmas!"

Everyone laughed and agreed that Christmas was indeed an awesome day. As Ryan pressed closer against Chet's chest, he wondered if the child could hear his heartbeat pounding out the words, "It's going to be all right, buddy. God's got our back—and He's never going to let us go."

THE END

New Hope® Publishers is a division of WMU®, an
international organization that challenges Christian believers
to understand and be radically involved in God's mission.
For more information about WMU, go to wmu.com.
More information about New Hope books
may be found at NewHopePublishers.com
New Hope books may be purchased at your local bookstore.

Please go to
NewHopePublishers.com
for the book club guide for *Return to Christmas.*

If you've been blessed by this book,
we would like to hear your story.
The publisher and author welcome your comments and
suggestions at: newhopereader@wmu.org.